Wolfhearted

Also by Kathy L. Brown

The Resurrectionist: A Novella (Sean Joye
Investigations Series, Book One)
Water of Life: A Novelette (Sean Joye
Investigations Series, Book Two)

Wolfhearted: A Novella

Kathy L. Brown

Otter Springs Publishing
St. Louis

ISBN 978-1-7330895-2-4

Otter Springs Publishing
St. Louis

To Mom, who thinks I can accomplish anything
to which I set my heart.

Acknowledgements

Thanks to my wonderful illustrator, Maria Ninfa (https://marianifa.mx); my mapmaker, Dave Schuey; my early readers, Dan Brown, Katie Brown, Carol Kruchowski, Lisa Parker, Deb Schuey, Brian Stamper, Kathy Van Voorhees, and LZ; and my creative support group, the Word Sisters.

Royal Hunting Villa, Tabzor

Seiðr/Curse

CURSE FORCES THE PATH, PULLS FATE'S
THREAD, AND TRIPS THE WICKED.

Freki's Edda, Aett Thurs, Stanza Four

R una dragged herself under a sickly yew, its dry branches spread low. "Shield me, friend." She flattened her wolf-shape against the frozen ground, melding her white fur against the frost-flecked grass while she licked blood from her wounded flank, chest, and paws.

It was late afternoon, judging from the long shadows that crawled across the landscape. Had she been captive in the stronghold an entire day? She gazed at the expanse of dead, clipped grass, precise shrub borders, and scattered clusters of young trees, bare and wizened. Beyond them rose a thick pine forest, marred by large swaths of tree stumps, evidence of clear-cut logging. A snow-covered road meandered through the woods and up the hill toward her. She sniffed the air. Trolldomr—evil sorcery—was at work.

A veil of snow covered the ground, and Runa smelled more snow to come. Fat clouds slid down the mountains from the west, encompassing the sky, and fog hugged the ground under the dead saplings. The fog might provide some cover if she asked nicely but taking shelter among the trees felt perilous. She knew in her heart that she must escape this place while she still had the strength. Yesterday, no, two nights ago, the drott—her high chieftain—had led the troop of hunters into an ambush. She'd be of no use to Drott Ulf if she were dead herself. She must heal, find help, and come back.

Bolting from the yew's cover toward the possible safety of the largest grove, Runa was but half the distance across the lawn when a tall figure, dark against the snow and fog, appeared from the copse. She knew him. Andries. A whimper escaped her lips as she retreated a few steps. Don't be a fool, she chided herself. Don't show weakness. She advanced, growling, "Let me pass, traitor."

"Runa, you *know* me." Andries sauntered across the frozen grass toward her, "I'm your friend. Let me help you and your people."

Her people—the kindred. How had she, weakest of her clan, alone escaped? What had he done with the drott and the earls?

He held his open hands out to his sides. "As you can see, I've no weapons. I could never defeat someone like you without a blade. You've always had the advantage over me, though too timid to use it."

Andries had convinced the kindred he was an honest man with useful metalworking skills, merely lost in the mountains. They'd taken him in, treated him as their own. But now he reeked of perverse sorcery.

"Where are the others?" Runa lunged, knocked him to the ground, and pounced on his chest.

Andries didn't fight. He smiled as she swiped and snarled at him, his breath a warm stirring of air against her fur. "My, you *are* in a bad way, aren't you?"

"Don't laugh at me." She managed a blow, but it glanced off his jaw.

He pursed his lips, his face a mask of false concern. "That's it? Your best attack?"

A memory intruded: screams and blood and a pile of pelts. Bile burned her throat.

4

"I'm entirely in your power. Kill me now," he said, "if you've the will. After all we've meant to one another." He embraced her, stroking her fur.

She snarled and aimed to sink her teeth into his throat but bit his cloak instead.

"Or," he said, "let me tend your wounds." He pushed her off his chest and nestled her on the ground. "Brew you a healing draught."

She struggled to escape. "I'll kill you."

"I beg to differ. I'm rather hard to kill now; your drott's quiddity—his very essence— roots itself in me."

"Liar."

"I *know* you can discern what I say is true. I am your liege lord, your drott, by the laws and customs of Frekigard."

Runa sniffed. Andries certainly smelled of Drott Ulf. Yet unnatural sorcery tainted the scent of the old king. Would Ulf have willingly yielded his marrow to Andries? No, this sorcerer must have stolen it, in some perversion of the ritual. "You . . . you're . . . wrong."

With a smirk, Andries patted her head and sprang to his feet. He took a strange object from his pocket: a long, thin box.

She crouched in the snow, curious, but more intent on which direction she should run. He slid the box lid back and forth, never actually opening it, his face twisted in concentration.

Her eyes darted across the horizon. Forest to the south and east. Tor formations—piles of massive boulders, rounded over centuries of wind, rain, and snow—to the north.

She'd just decided to take cover among the trees when a corrupted version of the rune Seiðr rose from the box. It wafted on the mist, then flared and hissed against the huge snowflakes that had begun to fall.

Andries scooped the symbol off the air and caressed it against Runa's throat. She yelped and leapt back; the rune was as a white-hot poker.

"Hush, hush. I'm sorry." He knelt before her, gathered her in his arms, and licked the burn on her throat. "Where else are you wounded?"

She scrambled away and ran into the forest beyond the park of dead trees and flower beds.

"Go now. You'll be back," Andries called after her. "Our fates are intertwined. In fact, you'll do me a great service this day. I'm your drott—will be at dawn, anyway. Like it or not, my will rules your heart."

Íor/Horse

H ORSE WINS THE RACE, PLOWS THE VALLEY, AND SPEEDS THE JOURNEY.

Freki's Edda, Aett Dómr, Stanza Three

The wolf coalesced in the late afternoon snow flurries, white against the black pines. Its scent alone was enough to panic Prince Paolo's stallion. The horse reared, bucked, and deposited him in a snowdrift before running off toward the river. A curse froze in his throat as the wolf approached, impossibly large and intimidatingly close. He was too entranced to reach for a weapon. The animal assessed and dismissed him in a moment, whether on sight, smell, or instinct he couldn't imagine. It turned and trotted away.

He lay in the snow a moment, lost in its grace, then, with a sigh of both relief and regret, began to scramble to his feet. But as he did, his face brushed up against something cold and wet hanging from a low bough.

A fist-sized heart dangled from a leather thong. He fell back, startled, then took a full breath and exhaled it slowly. Definitely a heart, real enough, and fresh. Blood still dripped off the tough membrane and glistened in the waning afternoon light. Strands of yellow fat wrapped the heart's surface. A leather thong bound the severed blood vessels, its knot twisted into a novel pattern. Was this some superstitious local practice to ward off ghosts? Entreat the Numinous Family? Cure meat? Widening his gaze and still alert for the shepherd—or priest, or butcher—who'd hung it there, he saw another heart on another tree. Then another. And another.

Waldo, his small spotted hound, had somehow landed on all fours when the horse dumped them. He bound through the snow to lick Paolo's face, sniff the air, and let out a howl. "Wooo, Wooo, wooolf hearts. The wolves' hearts hang here, master. How wicked. Ooooww."

Paolo wrenched his eyes away from the hearts. He was alone, save for Waldo. The dog looked up at him. "Did you speak?"

Waldo whimpered a bit, but he obviously couldn't talk. The prince laughed at his fancy and climbed to his feet. With the strain of movement, the freshly sutured musket ball wound on his thigh throbbed; he'd been on the battlefields of Hazzar, fighting the Voxkll invaders, that morning. A blood spot appeared on his trouser leg and grew larger by the second.

Paolo pressed hard on the wound. "Luca," he shouted after his horse. "You dolt, come back."

He looked down at Waldo. "I don't suppose you could fetch that idiot horse back here, could you?"

At the word "fetch" the dog took off into the woods, baying.

"No, no. He made toward the river." Paolo whistled for the dog as he strapped a pressure dressing to the wound, gathered his equipment, and righted the shako on his head. Supported by his scabbard, he limped after Waldo through a wood of bloody, dripping hearts. "Come when I call. You know better."

Waldo barked and reappeared to run around in circles and look at him expectantly. He didn't see the horse, but he did smell wood smoke and noticed a gray haze over the trees. "We must be close to the villa. Let's just follow"—he turned to look around in all directions—"the road." They were surrounded by fog and trees, the cold, wet air soaking his cloak and the winter-sleeping oaks' branches brushing his shoulders.

Yet they couldn't possibly be more than a few paces off the road, Paolo reasoned. He piled up a few rocks to mark the spot, slipped the hound a bit of jerky, and ordered him to stay while he made a methodical search of the area. All he found within ten meters of the cairn were more trees.

The fog cleared as he returned for the dog, and to his right he could see the afternoon sun dipping below the trees while gray billows of smoke floated along the horizon. "Ah, that way, then. Come, boy."

Waldo barked and bound ahead toward the setting sun. Paolo trudged after him. As he walked, he rehearsed the speech he'd written, huddled in the freezing gondola of an airship, while traveling home from the front lines. He'd need all the facts fresh in his mind when he made his appeal to the Auxumian People's Council.

"Honored citizens, courtiers, and my co-parents"—he bowed to the trees on the left—"your highness, my dear father"—he saluted the trees on the right. "Thank you for hearing my petition on such short notice." Each step pulled the muscles of his thigh against the sutures.

"In the matter of married royals serving the nation in the armed forces, who can forget Duke Francesco of Aufeer"—everyone, probably— "who in the year . . ." What *was* the year? That was the sort of thing he needed to look up and memorize. He was almost positive the essay he'd written on the duke, as an assignment from his old tutor, Master Andries, was still in his desk at the royal summer villa, Tabzor.

Paolo's appeal to the People's Council was not about his personal preferences. Well, not entirely. His duty to his country and fellow citizens was greater than unquestioning obedience to the king and council. He saw all too well that his role was pawn in some political machinations. Auxumian soldiers battled the Voxkll invasion force at that very moment. His place was at their side.

After about twenty minutes of crunching and bleeding through the snow, the puffs of gray smoke against the frozen sky looked much closer. Good thing, too. Night was almost upon him, and he had to do something about his leg, now quite numb from the pressure dressing.

But as night fell, more clouds rolled down the mountains, and soon they were wrapped in fog. He could no longer see the haze or smell the smoke. Snow had transformed the forest and obscured the trails Paolo knew well from many childhood summers.

He halted in a rocky glade. It was time to admit he'd lost track of which way he meant to go. Perhaps he'd made a wrong turn and crossed the border into Frekigard. For all he knew the whole Auxumia-Frekigard border was lined with animal heart warnings. Auxumia's neighboring nation was a secretive kingdom that allowed no visitors; few of its citizens ever ventured beyond its borders.

"Might as well make camp," he said aloud, mostly to hear a voice in the dark. It would have been a comfort if Waldo really *could* talk to him. "Those hearts back . . . I mean, over . . . no, definitely back there can't harm us. Rest easy."

With flint, steel, a pinch of gunpowder, and shaking hands he managed to start a fire, feeding it downed pine cones and dropped needles. The flames rustled and popped as resin ignited, and soon he was quite warm. "The mountain people are superstitious. As well as excellent cooks. Wild game heart is probably a real treat."

Blood had oozed from around the pressure dressing on Paolo's leg wound with every movement; he had to attend to it. He tossed his wet shako cap, pistol baldric, and other gear on a pile of evergreen branches. Loosening his breeches to inspect his thigh, he found the sutures had torn open in the fall. He made a hurried and poor job of surgery with the field sewing kit from his sabretache and bandaged the wound tight.

Sharing dried hyrax meat, dates, and a few sips of melted snow with Waldo, he huddled close to the dog. The clouds parted to reveal both moons over the trees, inspiring howls from deep in the woods. Waldo bayed in reply.

"And they are not wolf hearts," Paolo said. "They are . . . a game animal. Ibex, I think."

Despite the pain in his leg, he yawned, pondering the odds he'd freeze to death if he fell asleep. He wasn't all that cold anymore. He withdrew a packet of crisp documents from his uniform jacket's inner pocket: his discharge orders, a letter from the king, and a small portrait of his bride-to-be. A woman he'd never met.

He reread the orders again, "Paolo Vitela Yared, Second Lieutenant, His Majesty's Own Battalion, Fazil Brigade, citizen in good standing of Auxumia, and obedient subject, is hereby honorably discharged from said battalion, with full rights, privileges, and pension befitting his rank and length of service." He watched the flames dance and mentally rehearsed his arguments for staying in the army, married or not. He had one chance to present his case to the king, his other parents, and, most importantly, the council.

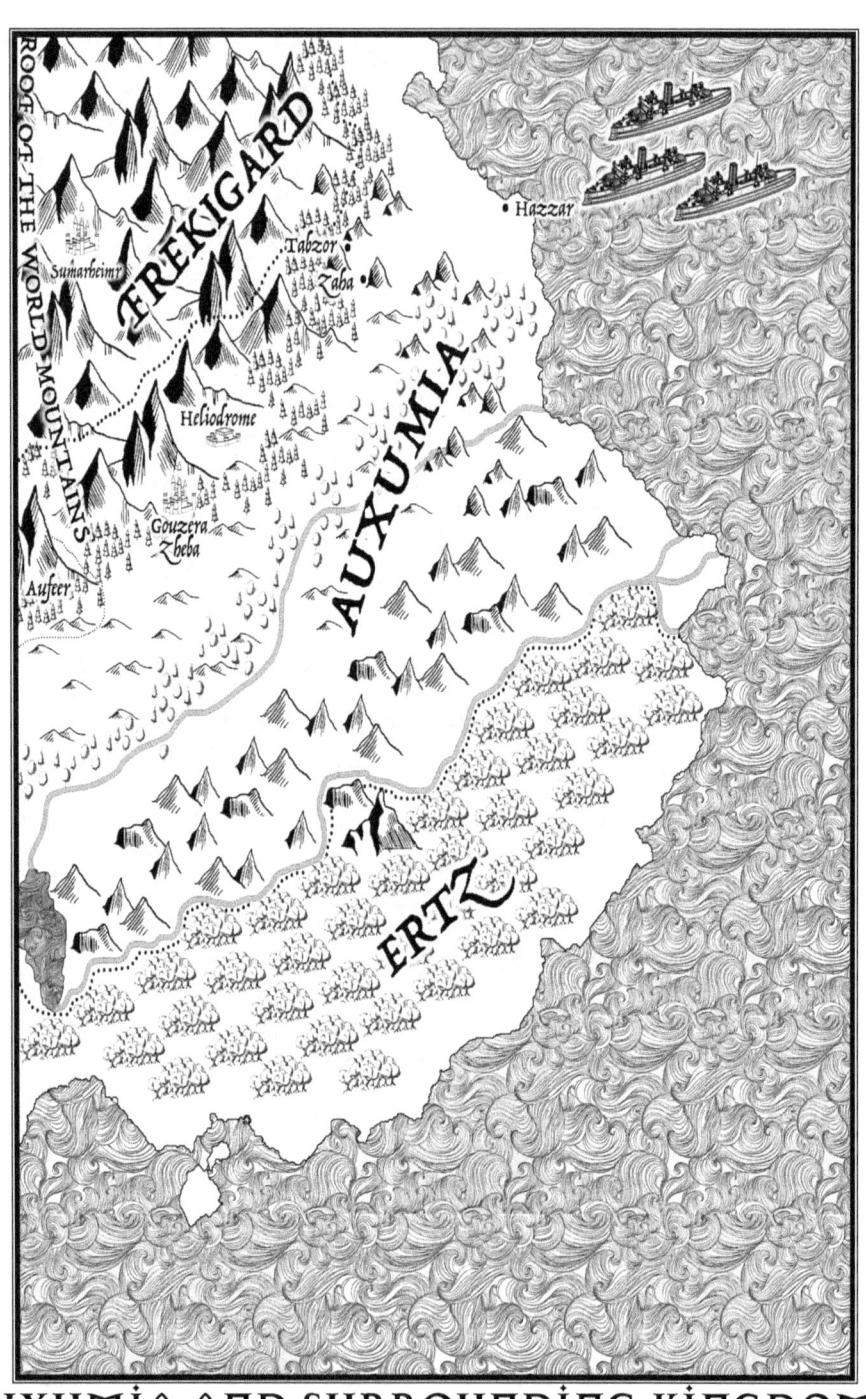

AVXVMIA AND SVRROVNDING KINGDOMS

Heit/Pact

Pact is a promise, a binding strap,
and a boon come due.

Freki's Edda, Aett Mergr, Stanza Five

R una smelled the campfire before she spotted the blaze in a glade surrounded by a thick stand of trees. She crept through the underbrush for a closer look at a small hound and a young stranger—clearly an utlendr—huddled near the fire. Earlier in the afternoon, she'd frightened a horse, who'd then thrown his riders: this same dog and man. Certainly not the sort of help she'd hoped to find.

She leaned back against the shaggy trunk of a giant pine and plucked a few wizen wild rosehips, overlooked by the birds, from a nearby shrub. "I thank you for this food, my friend," she murmured. Runa had spent hours licking her wounds while she tried to form a plan she could achieve alone. Recovering Drott Ulf's stolen life marrow—his essence and their kindred's legacy—was crucial to the Frekigardrs' survival. They'd all underestimated Andries, especially the drott himself. No. Especially me, she thought, right up until the end.

Andries had revealed his true nature, and she accepted that he had long deceived her. But she needed help to defeat him. Her only possible allies were these strangers; she'd found no one else. Why they camped in these woods in the middle of the night she couldn't imagine but gave thanks for them to Wolf-Mother. In woman-form she crept toward the firelight, hanging back among the trees.

Both the dog and man smelled half-starved and nervous. And wounded; one of them was bleeding. Wrapped in a dark cloak, the young man sat on a pile of pine boughs, the dog practically in his lap. Black hair frizzed around his forehead and was tied back at his nape. He held several parchments and stared intently at the fire as snow, unnoticed, coated his head. His face, bronze in the firelight, had strong bones and a crooked nose.

According to Andries, Skogr Utlendr, "Land of Outsiders," divided itself into many warring factions. This young man, by the cut of his cloak and the ribbon in his hair, appeared to be of Frekigard's adjacent nation, Auxumia. Like Andries.

She knew little of that language and hoped the young man had the common speech of the borderlands people. Squaring her shoulders like an earl about to scold her for some imagined infraction, Runa strode into the firelight just as he wadded up the parchments. She assumed a wide-legged stance, fists balled and planted on her hips to hide her trembling hands. "You are far from home, sir."

He jumped to his feet, grimaced, and promptly collapsed, dropping the parchment ball and a small painted image in the snow. "M-m-m-my good woman." He gestured to the fire. "Welcome. Please warm yourself."

Runa sighed in relief. He did know the borderland dialect, although spoke it poorly. So, the man was the one injured. He favored his right leg. She looked around. "*You* welcome *me*? Are these woods your kingdom?" One eye on the man, she stooped to fish his papers from the snow. The wadded parchment was pretty, covered in fancy script and gilded seals that meant nothing to her. However, she recognized the painting as Earl Marta, a noblewoman of Frekigard.

He stood again, shifting his weight to his left side. Silver buttons and braiding gleamed on the bright green and blue uniform he wore under the cloak. His brow knit in concentration. "Ah, give me a minute. You asked, 'Do you own the trees?' Well, one of my fathers does, yes."

"Your father is Auxumia's overlord?"

Once he figured out what she'd said, he winced as if she'd struck him. "No. I mean, yes, one of them is king. Far from an 'overlord,' believe me. But I didn't mean it like that." He waved vaguely to the southeast. "What I was trying to say is, this forest is part of our country. The border is about 100 furlongs to the north."

She shrugged under the tattered wool cloak she'd borrowed from an abandoned shepherd's hut. "A *disputed* borderland between Auxumia and Frekigard is more true, I believe. Tell your father that." Unsure of how much he comprehended, Runa took in his expression. Welcoming. But not intimidated.

He looked puzzled as he said, "Please sit here," Paolo pointed at his pine-bough mat, "not on ground. Better."

She handed back the parchment and portrait. "Why do you have this image?"

He hesitated, looked at the picture, then at her. Comprehension dawned across his face. "A marriage is—might be—" He waved the portrait around. "It's all political . . ."

She showed some teeth but took the pine-branch seat he'd offered. The dog groveling at her feet certainly understood her. She rubbed his muzzle and ears. "And who might you be?"

He whimpered a reply and promptly rolled over to offer his chest and stomach.

"What—" Paolo hesitated. He whispered to himself, "Just her, so singular. To bring. Bring, brings, brought." He started again. "What brings you out this night? Lost goat?" He hobbled over to a pile of dead tree limbs, at the ready to feed the campfire, and sat down on a log, then stowed the papers and portrait in an inner pocket of his short jacket. "Sorry I'm so rusty on the common dialect."

His gaze burned through the mask she'd donned. Could he smell her doubts? Among the kindred she was thought a small person, given to overthinking and hesitation. When things went wrong, most thought she was at fault, especially Earl Harald, the head of her own clan. She couldn't face her kindred as the sole survivor of a treacherous ambush. Even if she didn't die of the shame, they might well tear her apart in their grief.

Taking in the military emblems that bedecked his jacket, she considered how to best use his training. Or would *he* be the one to use weapons of war—to attack her?

His voice broke into her thoughts. "What . . . is . . . your name, ma'am? I'm Paolo."

"Runa." She tapped her chest twice in greeting.

"Runa." He stood and bowed. "Honored to meet you."

"And what brings *you* out this night? Lost yourself?"

Paolo thought her words over, then smiled. "I suppose. I made for the king's summer villa and got turned around."

"You're a soldier? I need a soldier this night."

"I am. A second lieutenant of the Fazil Brigade, His Majesty's Own Battalion," he said. "Well, I *was* until this morning. I aim to right the situation." He bowed again, then sat. "My class graduated the military academy early when Voxkll invaded. I'm with a horse artillery troop. My unit mans the six-pound guns Robusta and Libercia at Hazzar. At your service, ma'am."

The details meant little to her, but Runa could hear the pride in his voice. She stood and moved closer, hovering over him. "Good. Tonight, I attack and destroy a traitorous sorcerer. I'll let you help me, lieutenant."

Paolo looked up at her blankly. Comprehension spread across his face and he leaped up gingerly, favoring his weak leg. "You 'need to fight . . . some sort of . . . wizard'? In this day and age?" But before she could answer, he took a step back and narrowed his gaze. "Who is this person? What government orders the attack?"

She leaned in, inches from his face. "I order it," she said as she thumped her chest.

He glanced at his scabbarded sabre, sighed, and shook his head. "A policing action in a 'disputed borderland,' as you call it. We'd need an Auxumian arrest warrant. I'll ride . . ." he flushed, "I mean, I'll go back to Zaha and order out the town guard."

"There isn't time. The sorcerer must be destroyed by sunrise."

He thought on that awhile. "Why?"

"His trolldomr—evil spellwork— is weakest now."

Paolo smiled, then tried to hide it with a cough. He drew his features into a serious mask and nodded.

Infuriated, Runa, too, maintained a fierce guise to hide the tears stinging her eyes. She had to make him *want* to help her. "After sunrise it will be too late."

"Because . . . 'Magic?'"

She nodded and turned to warm her hands over the fire. A new tactic obviously needed, she wished she knew more about Paolo's kindred. She'd heard from Andries—assuming she could believe anything the sorcerer had ever said—that utlendrs generally placed great value on wealth, renown, and influence over other people and events. And while many kingdoms passed the crown to the leader's children, Auxumian succession did not.

This young man had no chance of ever becoming king. Some cousin of Paolo's would be the next ruler.

The flames snapped and crackled the pine cones, shooting sparks out to sizzle in the snow. She shook her head. Shouldn't a kindred's drott be its strongest and wisest member, their worth proven by food provided through the dark months and measured decisions to protect all the clans?

An Auxumian prince like this young soldier was most likely eager to gain the acclaim of his people. A weakness she could use. "I have just escaped from the sorcerer's stronghold. He has murdered my liege—the drott—and our entire troop of warriors—the earls."

"What? Murder?" The condescension dropped, and anger flared in Paolo's dark brown eyes. "The brigand." He grabbed his scabbard and limped back and forth across the campsite, waving it in the air. "He'll face the king's justice. If he survives; would that he doesn't, I'd just as soon—"

Good. He's ready to fight. Now to aim him at my enemy. Runa stood in his path and grabbed his shoulders. "This sorcerer is powerful. He exploits the marrow of all around him."

Paolo grew calmer as he positioned the scabbard's belt around his waist and buckled it. "Tell me his crimes. Exactly. The city guard commander will need to enter the charges in his warrant ledger."

No, no, no, she thought. We must strike now. She squeezed his arm and searched his face, staring deep into his eyes. As she offered up a prayer for the right words, the rune Andries had used to mark her throat throbbed. "He is the worst sort of man you'll ever meet, I fear. Or hope. Hope none could devise worse, but creative cruelty is the way of the outsider. Are you cruel, Lieutenant Paolo? Could you be if it suited your purpose or duty?"

He lowered his eyes. "I'm afraid I didn't get any of that." His back stiffened, and he squared his shoulders. "I'll arrest him on my own royal writ extraordinaire. How do I find him?"

"I will lead you. We must face him together to have any chance at success."

"Ah, 'together.' All right." Paolo filled a flask with snow and tightened knife sheaths at his wrists and boots. He looked her up and down.

Runa was well aware the shepherd's smock, loose breeches, and too-tight boots she wore looked far from battle ready.

Yet he didn't criticize her clothing, but merely said, "You'll need a weapon." He picked up another baldric, this one securing two pistols in holsters, and removed one of the guns. "You've used one of these? A flintlock?"

She shook her head. Not only had Runa not used a pistol, she'd never even touched one. To skulk from afar and attack one's enemies with artifice was cowardly.

He took a paper cylinder from a case attached to his belt, twisted it open, and shook a bit of black powder into a chamber he'd uncovered on the breech of the pistol. "Just use it to defend yourself."

"But—"

"Carry it half-cocked, so it can't fire accidentally." With a small rod he packed the pistol muzzle with the rest of the black powder from the cartridge, a lead ball, and a wad of paper.

"Half of what?"

"This position, see? Still ready to shoot, but a little jostle won't set it off." He fastened the flintlock's baldric across her chest. "The miscreant won't even get close."

Runa accepted it, knowing she'd never touch the accursed thing. "Give me one of your knives. You have four."

"Seven, actually." He shrugged. "If you want." Paolo removed a knife from under the right cuff of his jacket and buckled the sheath on her forearm. He primed and loaded his other pistol and slipped it into a flat leather bag hanging off his belt.

He took but a few minutes to break camp, and soon she was leading him and his dog through the woods. They hadn't walked far when he grabbed her hand. "I must prepare you—"

His touch surprised her, fingers rough and calloused and palm scabbed over with healing blisters. Andries had told her Auxumian earls were pampered fops, and Paolo's gaudy garments had confirmed his words. Now she wondered.

"An . . . unpleasant sight is up ahead." His dark eyes held her own, and her heart pounded, frantic to get away. "Someone has draped bloody entrails on the trees."

Runa swallowed and nodded. "I know. The sorcerer warded his lair."

"Warded?" He released her hand. "How—"

She turned away and pressed on as if she could leave his questions behind. Before long she caught the scent of the earls' blood hanging in the air, and an involuntary whimper escaped her heart. Waldo howled.

Soon they saw a heart dangling among a pine tree's thick needles and ripe cones. Beyond it, more trees wept over their bloody burdens. Runa glided silently from tree to tree; she held each heart against her cheek and whispered words of encouragement. Paolo and Waldo waited, the young man at silent attention, the dog cowering at his feet.

She pointed forward. "The barrier has a weak point, just ahead."

Óðal/Home

HOME IS WOLF'S HAVEN, THE MOUNTAIN
H PEAKS, AND THE KINDRED'S HEART.

Freki's Edda, Aett Dómr, Stanza Five

The forest thickened the further they walked, the pines older, taller, and huddled together. Paolo followed her as she skirted the wizard's "ward," as she called it, stumbling over rocks and surface roots that clung to the stony ground. Every jolt reminded him of his leg wound. Try as he might to be quiet, short grunts of pain and curses escaped his lips.

Runa turned around to glare and snarl, "Lieutenant, could you possibly be any noisier?"

While he didn't catch the meaning of all her words, her message couldn't be clearer. He snapped to attention and saluted, "As you wish, sir." She gave not even a hint of a smile. The Frekigardr was certainly hard to read. If they could just get on a proper path, the hike would be much easier. "Look, an ibex trail just over there," he pointed off to the left, "runs east and west. We could—"

But she'd continued the march, and eventually they broke through the tree line into a foggy, snow-covered glade. At last, he knew where they were: the northwestern border of the villa's grounds. He spotted several guard patrols silhouetted against the snow. Wood smoke hung in the air. Runa sniffed, then inched forward, ignoring the dark, ominous figures that barred their way.

Paolo advanced on the nearest guard from behind, dagger drawn and aiming to take them unawares, but he found he'd grabbed a small cedar in a headlock. All the forms he took to be guards were actually trees and shrubs. Those bigger shapes ahead would be the massive tor formation that marked the rear of the country villa's formal gardens. He knew them well, a fine place for children to climb, hide, and play army. "Now I know—" he looked around. Where had Runa gone?

Her form must be the moving one, up ahead near the piles of granite boulders. Paolo limped to her. "The ward is weakest here," she pointed at a tight passage between the towering rocks, "and your connection to this land is strong. Lead the way, and I'll be able to follow."

"Is this wizard in my house, then?"

Runa shrugged and linked arms with him. Even on the frozen air, he could smell her, like clean, fresh earth and as sweet as springtime. She closed her eyes and murmured words in a language he didn't know. As she did, the fog around them eddied in loosening loops and swirls ornate as lace. Soon their way was clear.

"Go." She pushed him forward.

The boulders loomed over him, leaning together to form a twisted stairway, the passage pitch-black in the foggy night. Guided by touch and memory rather than sight, he climbed over snags, ducked around turns, and avoided several sheer drops to the ground.

Stepping out into what Paolo knew to be the garden, the night was bright. Frozen crystals of fog mingled with wood smoke and glimmered in the starlight of the now-clear sky. Dark shapes dotted the lawn, a collection of deciduous specimens his papa had selected from all parts of Auxumia and tended as a public garden. Paolo had assisted with planting the saplings himself, eight or nine summers ago. The most tender plants, native to the balmy coast near Hazzar, thrived in a greenhouse built around a natural hot spring.

But as they approached the most proximal tree, Paolo realized it was dry and withered. Dead, not just sleeping through the winter. He limped from each to each and found them all in the same sorry state. And the larger specimens, many a native millennial tree, were nearly all gone, a wide swath of the grounds cleared to stumps.

Expecting Runa's rebuke for wandering off, he rejoined her. She patted his back. "The sorcery draws all the energy from the land."

His eyes began to water and burn. Damned smoke. "Puckle the magic"—he blinked and shook his head—"he's burning the trees." He wiped his eyes of sullied childhood memories. "Your sorcerer must have a blaze in every fireplace in the villa."

She shared no further opinion as she pushed on past the ghostly arbor toward the house, dead tree limbs reaching out to grab at them and hold them back.

Paolo couldn't believe what he saw up ahead; the fog and smoke must be playing tricks on his eyes. The house looked to be perched high in a thicket of oaks as if they'd grown up, around, and under the villa, pushing it into the air to create a twisted treehouse.

"Before we go in"—Runa's eyes were hard, gray stones—"grant me one boon."

She wanted . . . a favor? He thought that's what she'd said. "If it's in my power."

"The sorcerer stole many wolf pelts. From our troop of earls. If we're separated—"

"I won't leave your side." He looked up at the travesty of his home and moved ahead of her. "I should go first."

"Hush," she barked. "And listen. If we're separated or I'm killed, save the pelts and wrap one around each of the hearts that hang in the wood."

He wasn't sure if he understood her correctly. More of her magical beliefs? But someone had certainly damaged his family's villa and garden; he couldn't deny it. He saluted. "Any further orders, sir?"

"If I fall . . ." Runa pursed her lips. "It's hopeless." She looked at the sky and sighed. "You can't understand."

"Give me a chance."

"I'll think on it." She bent low and whispered a few words in Waldo's ear. The dog whimpered, but when she began to climb the central oak that held up the villa, he followed, scrambling and jumping from branch to branch.

Paolo was slowed by his injured leg but able to pull himself up. When he at last poked his head through the canopy of dead, rustling leaves, he found Runa bent over an iron-ring door handle, intoning strange words. A warm breeze began to stir the leaves. Waldo clung tight to a nearby branch and whined. He caressed the dog's head, and Waldo pressed against him, as if he would gladly climb into his arms like a pup again.

She scratched a sign on the door with the knife he'd lent her, then nicked her fingertip and traced her etching with blood. With a creak the door swung open. She entered and beckoned him to follow. Cold air greeted them as they stepped forward into the dark passage.

"This," Paolo looked around, "is the service entrance." He felt along the wall next to the door. "Should be a lantern right here." Although a bit rusty and only half full of coal oil, the lantern's wick was sound enough and cast a warm glow, bathing Runa in a pool of light.

She threw back her hood to reveal long, matted white-blonde hair and cheeks pink from the climb and the cold. His pistol and baldric were ridiculously incongruent draped across the loose shepherd's smock she wore. She acted like no shepherd he'd ever met.

Behind her, green, wooden planks lined the passage. Yet the villa interior had been rough, white plaster his entire life. "What has happened"—he touched the wall; it was, indeed, made of split pine logs, wet with sap—"to my house?"

Runa had bound forward but marched back to fetch him. "We must hurry." Her eyes glowed in the lantern light as she pointed. "His ritual room is this way."

Paolo retrieved his pistol from his sabretache. "I should go first. I've known this house my whole life." This might be her quest, but, by the Numinous Family, it was his home.

She tilted his face to look up at her, palms rough and warm on his cheeks. "He's perverted this place. He will use your love of home to trick you."

He bowed, just a slight head nod, and sighed. "Lead on, then, sir."

Runa didn't seem to need the lantern light, but Paolo certainly did. The passage was in no way the corridor he remembered. Eventually the timber-lined hall gave way to cold, wet, stone-block walls, and she stopped to wait for him to catch up. When he drew near, she pressed her fingertips to Paolo's lips, then pointed to the ceiling.

He thrust the lantern a bit further into the utter blackness. But he already knew what he would find. He could smell the acrid guano.

Bats, wings folded and eyes shut tight, huddled together, obscuring the corners and uprights of the tunnel. They wiggled, stretched, and squeezed their eyes more tightly shut in the light. Waldo sniffed at them then spit out a low "woof."

Runa crouched and bared her teeth in the dog's face. He groveled a bit, yet quietly, and trotted at her heels as she resumed walking.

Paolo followed. The bats straightened their ears and emitted mincing squeals to search them out and measure their party's size, strength, and threat. Waldo growled as the tunnel narrowed. It was just a matter of time before one of them disturbed the bats into flight.

As if his thoughts were prophecy, his shako's plume brushed against a beam, and the bats were upon them. "Take cover," he shouted as he shielded his face, but Runa didn't answer.

The air was as a living thing, a mass of flapping, wriggling fur and hide, the panicked animals fighting their way to perceived safety. They flew randomly and scratched Paolo's face and hands when they struck him. Their tiny bodies pelted his shako, tilting the visor over his eyes. He couldn't half see what he was fighting.

Waldo was on the attack; he leaped into the air to snap at his new enemies. Paolo dropped his pistol and drew his sabre to hack and slash at the bats with one hand and strike at them with the lantern in the other. A mound of bodies piled up at his feet, yet the onslaught continued.

What had become of Runa?

The light ebbed and flowed off the bats' wings as the lantern careened about. A large bat flew straight at his face. He slashed his sabre but missed, and the animal was on him, its odor only slightly less disturbing than the pain of its teeth puncturing his throat. The sabre and lantern clattered to the floor as he grabbed the bat and wrestled with its flapping leathery wings to pull it off. He stomped it under his bootheel, while the blood that dripped down his chest lured the rest of the flock to swoop and dive at him.

"Runa!" Just as the swarm drove him to cower on the floor, he caught sight of her. It was as he feared; she didn't even try to defend herself and instead stood stock-still under a small crack in the ceiling.

She intoned a song as she again punctured her finger with the knife, raised both hands toward the opening, and incised some sort of shape on the air with her bleeding finger. Bats swirled and swooped around her, moment by moment calmer, their squeaks deliberate and focused. Soon they followed the route she commanded up and out of the tunnel.

Paolo crouched in the guano, threw his shako across the corridor, and fumbled to relight the lantern. She strolled back toward him. "Sir, that was . . . I've never seen the like." But I've heard the like, he thought. Old, whispered tales of witches. Barely credible in this modern day and age. More likely Voxkll science; the invaders were frighteningly advanced. Magic is science we don't understand, Paolo reminded himself. Much had changed since the enemy first assaulted Auxumia's shores. Had Voxkll already made a secret alliance with Frekigard?

"I expect there's much you have yet to see." She brushed a bit of dirt or something worse from his face. She whistled for Waldo and advanced down the corridor.

Paolo retrieved his pistol from a guano pile and scabbarded his sabre. Suddenly exhausted, he struggled to his feet and trudged after Waldo, who trotted at heel beside Runa. The further he walked, the more difficult breathing became.

She halted her march. "I smell fresh blood." She looked at the dog, "Do you smell blood?"

Waldo gave what sounded like an affirmative sneeze, and they both looked back at him.

"What?"

"You're bleeding, lieutenant."

He touched his thigh. "Not anymore. I resewed the wound back at the campsite."

Runa grabbed his lantern and held it up to the neck wound. She sniffed. "Venom"— she pushed him to the floor—"must come out. Now." She tore open his jacket, waistcoat, and shirt and unsheathed the blade he'd lent her.

"Wait a moment." He touched the bite; his neck *was* swollen. And continuing to swell. In fact, he heard himself wheezing and could hardly inhale. Although he'd have liked to blame his breathing difficulties on her arm wrapped tight around his head, he felt his windpipe closing.

"Don't move," Runa said, her hair tickling his face as she bent over him. "Do you understand?" He struggled to escape. "Waldo, sit on his chest."

The dog obeyed, and Paolo tried to obey as well. Yet as he watched the knife approach his neck, his every nerve demanded he leap up and run away. Before he knew it, she'd scored the bite and covered it with her mouth to suck and spit out blood, again and again.

He felt half dead, rising to the Numinous Family's Garden on a cloud of bat venom, all too aware of her warm breath, smooth lips, and rough tongue's dance across the wound.

He wrapped his arms around Waldo and held the dog tight. "What have we gotten ourselves into?" he whispered.

"Oh, this is a fine pack, master," the dog replied. "Runa is a great leader."

Paolo closed his eyes, and all went black.

Úr/Mist

MIST HEALS THE EARTH, DAMPS THE FLAME, AND HIDES THE PATH.

Freki's Edda, Aett Thurs, Stanza Two

Runa followed the scent of dried herbs to what looked to be a kitchen. A fire crackled in a low, wide hearth. A cauldron dangled on a chain, poised to be swung over the fire as needed by way of a crane. Bellows, poker, and tongs hung on hooks drilled into the fireplace's fieldstones.

She stormed the pantry and grabbed likely bottles, flinging their stoppers across the room and sniffing the contents: Salt, yes, that would help. Spirits of hartshorn, certainly. She spotted plantain and madder drying from the rafters. "Friends, can you aid me? A man in my charge is sore in need of healing." Nearly spent, the herbs were glad to give what remedy they could. She stuffed a copper pot with the plantain and another with the madder root, murmured another thank you, and soaked the leaves with brandy and the root in water. I must heal Paolo because I need him to aid my fight, she thought as she set them on the fireplace's hob to warm, quickening the infusion process. Not because I like his company.

Her brews started to simmer, and she watched the bubbles stirred by the invisible forces Andries had once explained. Physics, he called it, not marrow of fire and water dancing into a new alliance. Science. How could she have been so blind? Andries had played the drott for a fool and somehow stolen his marrow. His very life, energy, and power. More than that—the marrow of all the drotts of the past. The kindred's heritage.

"Ancestors, grant me your healing wisdom." A new thought interrupted her prayer; perhaps all utlendrs studied physics. Paolo might have the same knowledge as Andries, which could be of more help to her than his battle skills.

Waldo trotted through the doorway, sniffed the remedy wafting on the air, and sneezed. He caught Runa's eye and paused.

"Approach."

He trotted over to sprawl on his back at her feet. She scratched his exposed belly. "How fares the patient?"

"He wakes, then sleeps again. I still smell the poison on him."

"Yes, bat venom spreads quickly, especially from neck wounds."

"Will he live?"

She checked the pots of simmering herbs. "I hope so." Runa took her concoctions off the heat. With the red madder dye, she sealed her intention by drawing the rune Úr on a shallow tray. Then she poured the plantain-infused brandy into the tray to cool. "The sorcerer of this place may have a stronger remedy to counter the poison." It would have been the height of foolishness to create a cloud of venomous bats without an antidote at the ready. And Andries wasn't a fool.

Waldo hopped up and wagged his tail. "Make him give it to my boy. Please? He's a good boy. He wants to help you."

Runa searched the kitchen's drawers and cupboards for cheesecloth. "I'm sure he does. But can he actually help or just get in the way?"

"Yes, oh, yes." Waldo jumped up and down in his excitement, knocking over the pot of madder dye. The blood-red stain spread across the oak heartwood floor.

"Quiet," she barked.

Waldo groveled. "My boy is quite fierce. I've seen it."

She strained the warm plantain brew into a pitcher. "I'll give him another chance"—she poured the remedy into a flask and stoppered it—"on your recommendation."

The dog cut a caper. "You won't be sorry, I promise."

Runa wrapped a portion of the wet herbs in an oilskin and stuffed it, along with the rest of the cheesecloth, the salt cellar, a bottle of the madder dye, and the spirits of hartshorn, into an empty lentil sack she'd found in a corner. "We'll see." She headed toward the doorway, and Waldo followed.

Gleipnr/Chains

CHAINS, FORGED FROM LINKS, BIND
PRISONERS IN THEIR CELLS AND
HEARTS TO THE PAST.

Freki's Edda, Aett Mergr, Stanza Three

A sensation of falling startled Paolo into wakefulness, and he found himself quite alone in a dim hall, moonlight through the high, clerestory windows streaming across a rough plank floor. His cloak was tucked up around his chin like a blanket, and he lay on Runa's cloak in the small dining room's service corridor, used when only the family was in residence at the villa. He listened for guard patrols and wondered where Runa and Waldo had gone. Paolo hoped she wasn't capturing the criminal without him.

Suddenly hot, he threw back his cloak and, although light-headed, hazarded to stand, clinging to the wall. As he took a few weak steps, memories flowed back. She had driven the bats out of that bizarre stone passageway. By singing to them.

Which made no sense; she must have used some sort of high-frequency signaling device. He'd attended a lesson about such technologia at the academy. Well, less a formal lecture and more like a set of assumptions and a hypothesis based on a heavily redacted captured blueprint. As far as the government had told the army, anyway, the device was still theoretical. But the invader's new technologia had attacked Auxumia on a daily basis for the past six months. Nothing would really surprise him. How Runa had gotten hold of it, that was the question.

Tired of waiting for her to come back, Paolo decided to search the building alone. He readied himself, knife sheaths secured and pistol drawn. He shuffled the length of the corridor, lantern left unlit, at last stumbling over the threshold of a wood-beamed archway to reach the wrought-iron spiral staircase that led up to the king's study.

Surely this—what did she call him?—sorcerer, a natural philosopher, he gathered, had sentries? Yet the house was quiet and felt empty. He climbed the steps, pausing every few moments to catch his breath and listen for a rush of guards or any sign of Waldo or Runa. As he climbed, the air grew warmer and less damp.

Paolo mounted the last turn of the spiral and stepped into a chamber transformed. The study's comforting smells of books, ink, and old paper were replaced with another set of odors, equally familiar and pleasant: the artificer's workshop back at the castle in Gouzera Zheba. The room was warm; a fire blazed in a hearth deep and wide enough to accommodate the tempering oven that filled it. The place smelled of coffee, wood smoke, and melting copper.

Refreshments were laid out near the fireplace: toasted flatbread, spiced butter, and grilled chicken morsels as well as blood oranges, his favorite treat. Fragrant steam rose from a chased-silver coffeepot. A figure was hunched over the king's desk, which was laden with rolled parchments and stacks of diagrams. The tall, strongly built man was intent on a slide-rule calculation, but at the sound of Paolo's bootheels on the heartwood floor, he looked up, face beaming. "Welcome, welcome."

Paolo was sure he knew this fellow. He couldn't remember from where, though. That fact troubled him quite a bit; he must be more impaired by the bat venom than he realized. After appraising the stranger's threat potential, Paolo surveyed the room for hidden guards or useful weapons.

"I knew you'd come back."

What an odd thing to say. Still, the man didn't appear to be armed, hostile, or guarded. Bracing himself against any telltale winces and willing a confident stride he didn't feel, Paolo took a step toward the stranger. He couldn't shake the conviction that he knew this man well.

As he opened his mouth to challenge the squatter, a voice from behind him interrupted, "Yes. I'm back. To feast on your heart." Runa glowered from the doorway at the man. Waldo bared his teeth and growled.

"And you've brought the prince," the man said to her, "just as I asked you to."

She sputtered a protest, but the familiar stranger made a calculation with the slide rule and gestured at Runa with it. "Hush now. I must talk with my old friend."

Her shoulders slumped, and she stood quiet.

Turning to Paolo, the man continued, "My dear, dear boy, I'm so happy to see you again." The ruddy-cheeked stranger's thick gray hair was streaked with white. A loose quilted vest of deep blue hung over the simple, yet finely woven, woolen tunic he wore, laced at one shoulder with leather thongs and cinched at the waist by a wide belt with a gleaming, ornate buckle.

Laugh lines creased the man's face. "Surely you remember me, don't you?" He frowned a mock pout. "I'm hurt."

"Master Andries?" Paolo bowed, everything else, including Runa, momentarily driven from his mind. Here stood the royal artificer, his favorite tutor. More than tutor. His workshop had been both classroom and refuge from the tumult of brothers, cousins, and courtiers. And the inconsistent attention of his parents. "You made my tin soldiers." He uncocked the pistol and tucked it in his sabretache. "I've not seen you since——"

"Too long, too long. I've made many things other than your toys though none brought me more pleasure." Master Andries strode around the desk to the coffee table. He offered the refreshments with an elaborate gesture, grinning all the while. "Come have a bite to eat." He poured coffee into a demitasse cup. "I've all your favorites, and I know you must be hungry." Master Andries held tongs over a sugar bowl and looked over at Paolo. "Still have that sweet tooth?"

He shook his head. He'd spent hours with this man on a daily basis, as far back as he could remember. Master Andries was always there. Until, suddenly, he wasn't.

"Ah, you're a man full grown now." He offered the cup to Paolo, and his eyes flicked over him, head to foot. "You were just a child when I had to leave."

Paolo made no move to take the coffee. Master Andries shrugged, set it down at the place setting opposite him, and then filled a saucer with water and put it on the floor. Waldo growled.

"What . . . why are you in our house?" He scanned the room for some sign of royal commission, which by law should be posted in any government facility. "Did mother or one of my fathers send you here? Or the council?" He took a few steps toward the coffee table, clinging to the furniture and trying his best not to hobble. "So you could have more room to build your inventions?" Surely Master Andries couldn't be the wicked "sorcerer" Runa had accused of so many crimes.

His old teacher sighed. "It's difficult to explain the disagreements I had with your parents. I but sought to advise them toward upright conduct in the best interest of Auxumia's people. And you, my boy, most particularly, *your* best interests. King Gian is a rather short-sighted 'leader,' and Lady Asha overprotective of her youngest child."

Paolo nodded. Mother hated his plan to make a career in the army. He'd bet his dog and his horse as well she was behind the army discharge, using the marriage plans as an excuse.

"Your . . . other father"—Andries pursed his lips, like he'd just bit into a green persimmon—"actually agreed with me in principle."

"Agreed with what?"

"My boy, your potential. Your destiny for true greatness."

"Papa said that?" He tried to picture Sir Frederick breaking off from his garden long enough to discuss Paolo's future. He couldn't imagine it.

"My efforts exploded in my face, as it were." He wrapped a bit of chicken in flatbread—wheat bread! Master Andries had actual bread— and motioned Paolo toward the chair opposite him. "Please sit, young sir, and enjoy your coffee. I've studied natural philosophy, long and hard, as a true leader needs to do. I want to talk to you alone."

Paolo glanced back at Runa, who blinked her eyes and flexed her muscles as if she'd just woken up. Master Andries again drew a few symbols in the air with the slide rule. Out of the corner of his eye, Paolo could see the sigils glow in the firelight. The teacher made a flinging motion at the woman, and her shoulders slumped again. "You've earned high marks at the academy, I'm proud to hear."

"Don't do that to her," he said. "Please."

Master Andries' eyes flashed for a moment, then he resumed his smile. "I did nothing. She has entered the meditative, restful state her people frequently seek out. Resets their energy flow."

Paolo nodded. He wasn't entirely sure of what he'd seen and had to admit he knew little of the Frekigardr people's ways.

"But," Master Andries' face grew solemn, "I hear you haven't avoided the moral turpitude of modern Auxumian life. I taught you a better way."

"About what?" As wonderful as the artificer's shop had been, he recalled the master droning on about "temptation" and "sins of the flesh." No one else Paolo knew, not his parents nor even his priest, applied pious deliberations to biology. "Oh, I guess you were talking about sex back then. Quite over my head at the time."

"Well, since you're an adult now, let me—"

Before Master Andries could start up the parable of the lewd whore and the foolish young cadet, Paolo slid into the offered chair. "Do you invent war machines here? To defeat the invaders?" *That* was an exciting idea. Paolo longed for the coffee. If he weren't just so tired and weak. Too weak to pick up a cup.

"Do you know another word for 'invader'? Liberator."

Paolo stared at the man. What had happened to him? "Voxkll has 'liberated' thousands of our citizens into an early grave."

From across the room Runa growled, "Now, you die," as she tried to stumble forward but sank to her knees instead. Waldo took up barking.

"We'll talk more later." Master Andries stood, still smiling. "Alone."

At the movement Paolo instinctively reached for his pistol. Master Andries laughed, "Ah, boys and their guns. How I've missed you." He shook his head and sighed, then produced a small blue flask from an inner vest pocket. "This might interest you, Your Grace. An antivenom elixir. Much longer, it will be too late."

Paolo pointed the pistol and struggled to focus. This man looked like Master Andries. The shop smelled like his shop. Yet something was wrong. Was it his sympathy with the invaders? Or Runa's insistence this man had murdered her party?

He hauled himself to his feet. "Sir, I must detain you for questioning." As he lunged across the table at the man, she rushed forward. He grabbed his old mentor, but Master Andries seemed to melt in his arms. Paolo and Runa found themselves clutching nothing at all except each other. Waldo let out a howl.

Logi/Fire

Fire tears apart all, forges anew,
and burns in the prideful heart.

Freki's Edda, Aett Thurs, Stanza Six

G asping for air, Andries collapsed on a bench in the great hall. The edifice's only space sufficient to house his steam engine and scientific equipment, most of its hideously overornate rococo furnishings were either pushed back against the walls or long since burned as fuel. A cold wind whistled through cracks in the ebony outer doors, their panels carved with horses, hunters, and dogs cavorting in an improbable landscape of steep mountains, wild rose bushes, and acacia trees.

Despite the moist heat off the engine, Andries shivered in the draft. Warm wolf pelts, the final physical remains of his captives, lay nearby, but they stank of blood and defiance.

"Impressive, don't you agree? Projecting our essence as we did." He was alone with the pelts. He'd draped the finest—fur glossy, a thick motley of gray, black, brown, and white—on an oversized sandalwood chair cushioned in bright green tapestry and carved with crocodiles and snakes. King Gian favored it, he recalled. "I can feel you in my heart, Drott Ulf," he said to the pelt, "or at least your quiddity. Your spirit is confused, very confused."

The illusion experiment to reach out to Paolo had cost Andries a great deal of energy; although he'd transferred Drott Ulf's power to himself, he couldn't employ it just yet. Not until the old king gave up the struggle.

He needed to write up his observations. He needed to sleep. But the drott's quintessence kept up a pitiful howling within him. "Silence," he shouted at the pelt-draped chair. "You brought this on yourself. Hording power for anathematic practices when the realms are in dire need—"

Andries' low back twinged, then cramped. He stretched out on the stone floor and closed his eyes. He willed his body to relax into the cold's embrace and his soul to ignore the wolf essence coursing through his energy channels. Save Auxumia, yes. Then Frekigard. And secure Paolo's future. The boy was too naïve, a lamb among the wolves at court, to ever do what was necessary himself.

By the Watching Eyes, it was good to see his protege again. Hadn't he turned out well? Tall, handsome, and more intelligent than his whole family put together. The boy was exceptional, even as a child. Andries had long prayed the king would acknowledge and cultivate the prince's abilities and his mother would impose the discipline and structure a child needs to excel. He had even appealed to their paramour, "Papa," as Paolo insisted on calling him, for support.

But, instead, they'd grown jealous of Andries' influence over Paolo. King Gian, ever the suspicious hothead, had even accused him of an unnatural attachment to the prince and put him out. His back tightened again, shooting pain down his right leg. He breathed into it deeply and let out the pain with the exhale. He should have known better; a polygamist and sodomite like Gian will always bring any noble, fine sentiments down into his own muck.

Without opening his eyes, Andries spoke to Drott Ulf's pelt. "King Gian and the court will have to respect the boy, the prince, I should say, after the treatment. With your earls' quintessence—"

Deep within him, Drott Ulf snarled and twisted. Andries cowered a moment before the angry beast, then he leaped up, grabbed the drott's pelt, and wrapped it around himself. "*I* am the power now." He marched to a credenza he'd turned into a laboratory bench, tore open a notebook, and refigured a page of calculations. "My extraction method works, as you well know, dear Ulf. Your quintessence successfully transferred to me. The treatment will work safely on others. I can transform *any* soldier to overcome mundane limitations. My dear young prince will benefit first. Voxkll victory and a holy moral order for Auxumia is within our grasp."

Andries draped the pelts front paws over his shoulders and crammed its face atop his head as a hood. "Soon I'll get the prince away from that damned Runa. She's played her part." He tied the back legs together, low on his hips. "Well, almost. One more procedure."

Hugga/Embrace

EMBRACE QUICKENS THE HEART, COMFORTS THE MOURNFUL, AND BINDS THE PACK.

Freki's Edda, Aett Thurs, Stanza Five

M aster Andries had slipped away somehow, probably through a hidden door, but Runa was a real presence in Paolo's arms: alarmingly real. And she clung to him too, her embrace firm as her fingers traced the lines of his shoulders and neck. Looking for direction in her cool gray eyes, *he* certainly wasn't going to break the moment, squatter on the loose or not. He caressed the small of her back and tightened his arms around her waist to pull her closer.

Runa released him and stepped back. "You *are* a distraction, you know."

"Sorry," he said. "I could say the same about you. Sir." Actually, she was much more than a distraction. Of course, he'd had crushes before, intense bouts of puppy love and the occasional brush with an eager barmaid or stable boy, which some court functionary generally put a stop to right quick. Or the romance ran its course, dissolving in tears and mutual regret.

Around him, the workshop began to fade like a chalk drawing left out in the rain. To avoid the scent of her hair, the curve of her cheek, and the flutter of ridiculous happiness her touch inspired, he limped around the room, lighting the coal-gas lamps. Soon the place was but the king's familiar, book-lined study.

Runa wasn't a distraction. Or a crush. He'd never met anyone like her.

He watched her rummage through a burlap sack she'd brought with her, burnishing her image into his brain for later. A strongly built blonde, long hair tangled and festoon with twigs, she stood a bit taller than he. Dark bruises mottled her throat and blue smudges creased her eyes. Her tan, heart-shaped face showed a few faint lines around her mouth and was marked with healing cuts.

So beautiful. Although she carried herself proud, he'd noticed it seemed to take a great effort to do so. Master Andries had hurt her, badly, Paolo realized, tamping down a flash of rage. His old friend would pay. At the proper time, he'd pay.

"Drink this," her voice interrupted his vendetta plan. She offered him an amber flask.

He sniffed it, curious as to what Runa thought he needed to drink. His fathers' favorite brandy, he thought, with an herbal, green undertone.

"It'll bind the poison. Slow its effect." She pulled him closer—"Drink it all"—and pushed the flask against his lips—"now."

"Your sorcerer is my old tutor, who left the court when I was a child." Paolo had to get control of the situation. And himself. "A man well known to me." He took the flask from her hand and trailed a finger over the bruises along the front of her throat. "Did he hurt you?"

She gulped and brushed back a lock of matted hair from her face. "He has murdered my drott, my clan chief, and a half dozen earls. My scratches aren't important."

"I disagree. And for any legal action, I need to collect proof of Andries' guilt."

Runa pushed his hand, still holding the flask, toward his mouth. "Please."

Well-trained from too many barracks drinking contests, he tossed back the brandy in one gulp. "And to know the details of your plan." He

60

wiped his mouth with the back of his hand and leaned against the desk to take some weight off his wounded thigh.

Her eyes flashed, Waldo cringed, and Paolo felt like joining him to grovel at her feet. But he knew he was right. While she acted like a military officer, she wasn't actually *his* commander. He wanted to trust her. Yet he couldn't trust blindly. At least they could talk with greater ease now; he had remembered more and more of the mountain dialect as the evening progressed.

Despite her obvious anger, Runa didn't shout at him.

She perched on the desk's edge, her shoulder barely brushing his. He swallowed, hard, over a lump in his throat.

She spoke softly in his ear, "Don't you find it strange your old teacher is camped in your house? Surely you remember something about his departure from your kingdom?" She hopped off the desk and pulled some bottles, gauze, and an oilskin-wrapped parcel out of the sack.

"I'll admit it *is* odd to find him here." Quite odd. Paolo had visited the villa just six months earlier, on leave before his deployment to the siege of Hazzar. Master Andries certainly wasn't in residence then.

She pulled his jacket and waistcoat back off his shoulder and began to unbuttoned his shirt. He gulped. "Ah, sir. What're—"

Runa loosened the bandage on his neck. "This might sting a little." She drenched the wound with liquid from one of the bottles.

Pain shot through his neck and down his arm—"By the Mother's bleeding bum"—but also shot down all amorous impulses. He grabbed the bottle out of her hand.

"Don't be such a child," she said, snatching it back. "Go on. 'It *is* odd to find him here . . .'" she pried the lid off a small jar.

"Yes, odd. I don't know whether anyone would have told—" Next, she literally rubbed salt in the wound. "Puckle me!" He jumped up and hobbled away, but she dragged him back and shoved him to sit on the desktop for her continued ministration.

"Hush. What should your earls have told you?"

The burning subsided a little. "If Andries was working on secret war machines here, I don't know that they'd say." Actually, he was pretty sure they wouldn't tell him. It wouldn't have occurred to the People's Council to include any of the many minor royals in their deliberations.

Runa unwrapped the oilskin and extracted a wad of wet weeds, then slapped the herbal compress onto his neck. She proceeded to probe and pack the wound with it. Paolo found it the least unpleasant of her remedies.

"Hold this in place while I wrap it."

As he did, he thought on his old tutor. Andries was in his workshop as usual during his ninth summer, right before he went away to military school. A few months later, home during the winter holidays, no Master Artificer was in the workshop and no one wanted to talk about him. "I haven't seen Andries in over ten years."

"And where has he been?"

"I don't know."

"I do." She tied off the bandage, her fingers lingering on the cloth to trace yet another of her magical symbols with a dab of red dye. "At least for the past five years. Our border patrol found him, weak, half frozen, and near death. We took him in. I nursed him back to strength and health myself." She tapped Paolo's thigh. "Shall I dress this wound as well?"

At her touch, his leg twitched like that of a galvanized frog and knocked over a tiny porcelain goatherd figurine from the corner of the desk. "Gods, no, no. It's fine," he said as he rescued the object from a fall.

She jerked her hand away from his leg and frowned, stepping back.

Now I've insulted her. He blabbed the first words that came into his head. "Aren't you too young to be a doctor?"

She didn't reply at first, then at last said, "I had to learn to be a healer." She bit her lip and turned away, blinking.

Now I've stepped in it, he thought. "Runa?" He touched her elbow. "I'm sorry. Whatever I said."

"You said nothing. Hartshorn fumes in my eyes," she sniffled as she rolled her shoulders and pushed her white-blonde curls back from her face. "I was about your age and knew very little of healing. The drott ordered me to do it. To nurse an utlendr . . . was meant to be a punishment." She narrowed her eyes and curled her lips at the memory. "But I kept Andries alive."

Paolo didn't entirely understand her story, but her message was clear. "The drott," he said through clenched teeth, "often made you do things you didn't want to do?"

Her eyes grew red and moist, and she paced the room, chewing a fingernail. "At times"—she spit the words out like a particularly bitter remedy—"Earl Harald, my clan chief, would complain about our bad luck. The drott had to find a cause."

"You don't have to make excuses for your king." He pressed the goatherd figurine into Runa's hand and pointed at the fireplace. "Go on. It will make you feel better."

"What will?"

"Break something." He grabbed a crystal paperweight made into the image of a crouching lioness and threw it into the hearth to shatter against the firebrick.

She looked in turn surprised, alarmed, and then puzzled.

Paolo grinned at her. *He* felt better, at any rate. What else? He grabbed a marble owl-shaped bookend and hefted it. Substantial. "So, you'll choose my spouse *and* career, will you?" he asked it, then flung the owl after the lioness. It smashed against the andirons in a dozen chunks.

She'd been watching him, a worried look on her face, but now a smile tugged at the corners of her mouth to reveal deep dimples. "*I* carry the clan's ill-luck?" Runa heaved the china ornament into the fireplace. "The chief's choices have no part? Me alone?" She laughed and snatched a brandy snifter off a credenza and threw it as well. "That *is* satisfying."

"Go ahead. Break some more of the king's belongings."

"That's enough." She plopped onto a blood-red brocade chair and sighed. "Eventually Andries' arrival was thought a good portent. Your old master taught us much about Skogr Utlendr."

"What? Or, where?" Paolo sat on the chair arm. Runa cocked her head and looked him up and down but didn't shoo him away.

"Skogr Utlendr, 'Land of the Outsiders.' Any place beyond our mountains. Your kindred and other realms as well. Andries has travelled far. He also knew the working of metals into sharper, lighter, yet sturdier tools. Healing draughts. And, of course, songs and stories of wonder. The young ones were enthralled around the fire each night."

"So, he recovered among your people and stayed on awhile to teach." That much rang true; Master Andries was always eager to perform. "Where'd he go next?"

She looked away. "Well, nowhere. It is forbidden."

"What is forbidden?"

"Anyone from Skogr Utlendr who climbs Hrimpurs or Flago Jokull into our lands cannot ever leave it. Yet he did leave."

"Climbs what?"

"The mountain ranges. He'd strayed into the 'Glacier Giantess' here to the east when we first found him."

"We call those mountains the 'Roof of the World,'" Paolo said, pointing to a framed map of Auxumia on the wall. As he did so, her words sunk in. "Did you say, 'forbidden to leave?' I'm to marry a Frekigardr earl soon." Had King Gian discharged him from the army because he'd soon be a prisoner in Frekigard?

"And you'll be forbidden to leave." She shrugged, like the fact wasn't particularly important. "Last night—no, two nights ago, Andries slipped out of the drott's settlement at Sumarheimr."

Well, such a law would make a military career after the marriage difficult, to say the least. He pushed aside that problem and wrenched his focus to the one at hand. "Both moons rose well past midnight," he said. "A good time to escape."

"Our best hunters"—she touched his forearm and left her hand to rest there—"don't worry. Earl Marta wasn't in the party." Her gray eyes, so cool, even cold, teased him. "Led by the drott himself, pursued." She bit her lip. "The trail was obvious. Too obvious, in my opinion. But the earls seldom listen to me, and Drott Ulf was eager for the kill."

"Probably angry at being fooled."

"Anger clouds judgment." She looked away. "Our party rode into a trap. His curses bound us. I awoke, alone, in this keep."

"Curses?" Charming, the way she always jumped to a supernatural explanation. He leaned in closer and rested his arm across the back of the chair. "Maybe some sort of poison. Delivered by technologia new to you."

Runa thought on that. "Does it matter?"

"Perhaps not. Magic is science we don't understand." Master Andries had often said so.

She stood. "With your 'technologia,' are there forces you can't see with your eyes or touch with your hands?"

"Of course." His thigh wound was throbbing again, but he stood as well. "Electricity, magnetism, thermodynamics, for instance." He pointed at the cheery light of the sconces around the room. "Gaseous forms are often invisible."

Runa leaned in closer, her breath warm against his cheek. "And those forces can be petitioned by those who know how."

"Sure," Paolo gulped. "Technologia." The room suddenly felt too warm.

Annoyance flashed in her eyes but was just as quickly replaced by a chuckle. "Words." She stepped back. "Do you believe me now?"

"How could he"—Paolo waved his arms around to indicate the villa—"do all this in one night?"

"I suspect he had help. Either utlendrs set up this stronghold, or—"

"Someone in your village has been letting him out."

Her shoulders slumped. She threw herself back in the chair, drew up her legs, and hugged them. She seemed much smaller, somehow.

Paolo sat in the chair with her and wrapped his arm around her shoulders. She didn't push him away. Waldo padded over to whimper and lick her boots.

Her story about Andries was plausible. And he couldn't fault a prisoner for escaping, no matter how kindly he'd been treated. Although his old tutor should have gone straight to the nearest border post or the militia barracks at Saba when he escaped, rather than ambush and attack his pursuers alone. And hurt Runa. "So, we are here to rescue your party's survivors?"

She opened and closed her mouth several times before spitting out, "In a way."

"Either we aim to save them, or we don't."

"He claims to have killed them all, and I believe him. Yet there might be a chance—"

Paolo gave her arm a squeeze. "Then we shall gather evidence and arrest him. He will face the king's justice."

"He has stolen the drott's marrow, and the light of the new day will seal that power to him. I must recover it by dawn. The fate of not just my kindred, but all kingdoms of this land are at stake. Yours included."

His heart believed her before his brain could translate her words and form the obvious rational question: How did one steal another man's power? He sat on the chair arm, silent.

"If I fail," she stood and took both his hands in hers, "your dog and you are the only ones who can stop him. Promise me you will do whatever it takes."

"I promise. Just tell me how."

Ár/Reaping

REAPING IS THE HARVEST, THE FRUIT OF THE SOWING, AND LOVE'S REWARD.

Freki's Edda, Aett Mergr, Stanza Four

Paolo's brown eyes shone with worshipful admiration that Runa had to admit she enjoyed— bright, insightful, and eager to help. None of the kindred or even her own clan admired her. They merely tolerated her, a useful target of blame in hard times. He'd been through great hazard on her behalf this night, without any duty at all to do so. His short jacket, encrusted in his own blood, was torn at the shoulder, a silver epaulet dangling by a thread, and he'd lost his cloak and silly plumed hat in the course of the evening.

She had begun to trust this utlendr, yet she doubted he'd ever accept the ritual required to secure the drott's marrow for the kindred's legacy. At best, if Andries killed her, he might be able to save the hunting party by restoring the pelts to the severed hearts. Runa sighed and squeezed his hands. "Later." She stood. "We must find the sorcerer."

He jumped up off the chair, grabbed her shoulders, and looked her square in the face. "Enough with the hints and threats. Cut the twaddle and tell me what you need done."

"Our ways," she whispered, "are not yours."

"In a few weeks I'll be married into your people."

She nodded. "Our life marrow—"

"Your power?"

"You mean strength . . . might?" She shrugged. It wasn't accurate, but the word would have to do. "Our 'power' lives here," Runa struck her chest. "The ruler's heart carries the lineage of all the rulers who came before. The marrow is passed from one to the next."

Paolo nodded. "Some sort of ceremony, I imagine."

"There is a ritual. But it is more than that. A real, physical bond."

His eyes had a far-away look, and he stroked the wisps of beard on his chin. "And?"

"The old drott's heart . . . " She paused, then flung the words in his face—"is consumed by the new ruler. And thus, the line continues."

He blanched. "So, you think Andries has *eaten* your king's heart?"

Runa started to nod but stopped herself. She didn't think that. The sorcerer boasted the drott's marrow, true, yet he also stank of trolldomr. He hadn't followed the customs properly at all. "He has done something *unnatural* to the drott to gain his life marrow. I know as much."

Paolo slipped his pistol from its baldric that she wore across her chest, inspected its workings, and took aim at the tall floor clock across the room. "Thus, he dies."

"No. I mean, yes." She grabbed his arm and lowered the weapon. "If you merely kill him, the line of our drotts' power will die with him. My only hope is to consume the sorcerer's beating heart and take the marrow back to my kindred."

Looking deep in thought, he stared at a life-sized portrait of a richly dressed woman on the wall. Runa waited. "So, you would be king," he said at last.

"I would be drott," she agreed. "Until someone stronger defeated me." Which wouldn't be long at all.

"And, in turn, ate *your* heart?"

She could only nod. Although Runa knew precious little of Auxumian ways, she knew Paolo could never understand, even if he married Earl Marta and lived with them the rest of his life.

The tall clock's gears clicked away the moments, and wind rustled dead tree branches against the window. Tiny feet scampered in the corner of the room. Waldo pounced, and she heard a squeak cut short as the clock chimed once.

Paolo cleared his throat. She didn't know what she expected to see in his eyes, but not—Irritation? Impatience?

"I think you would be a good king," he said. "But let's cross that bridge when we come to it. And thank you. I appreciate *finally* knowing what I volunteered for. To be clear: My commission is to find and capture Andries. Then you eat his heart."

Runa felt he was angry. "I should have—"

"Been honest about why I was to abandon my duty to king and country and help you?"

"You are not—"

"If I get killed I am."

He would either choose to help her, or he wouldn't. Runa was almost relieved his actions were now out of her hands. She grabbed her sack of remedies, signaled the dog, and headed toward the door. "He can't be far away." Andries couldn't have cast such a convincing illusion from any great distance. "And if he didn't lie about the bat venom antidote, we need to take it from him."

"Wait just a minute."

"Go back to your king, lieutenant. I'll kill the sorcerer myself."

"I said I would help you. And I will." Paolo began to search the hearth. He ran his hands around the fireplace, muttering, "Sliding doors? Hidden panels?"

Runa crossed the room to tap his shoulder. The loose epaulet, a brocade crouching lioness, came off in her hand. "He was never here at all," she said, "The whole scene was an illusion to distract us. To slow our search for his real lair."

"Like with a lantern projector?" He turned his search toward the mantel stonework. "I suppose it could be hidden in here." He ran his fingers along a mortar seam. "Though I don't see how the mechanism could be made small enough."

"We're wasting time." she glanced out a window to judge the position of the moons. The sky had clouded over, and snow was falling. "Which we have precious little of." Runa moved again toward the door with Waldo right behind her. "Are you coming?"

Paolo ceased probing the joints between the stones with a letter opener. "There might be guards." He limped to the doorway to join her. "I can't believe he's here alone."

She nodded, pressed the lioness emblem in his hand, and peeked around the corner to survey the corridor. She smelled nothing except dust and fireplace ash, and all she saw was a diffuse glow in the distance. They crept toward it, wary of patrols, but when they found the staircase, they could see the light's source was from below. They hurried down flight after flight of steps. "This villa only has three levels," Paolo said. "How can there be so many stairs?"

"Well, they seem real enough." At last, they reached the foot of the stairs. Runa felt they were deep underground, the weight of the forest above stifling, suffocating, and unnatural.

Ahead of them was an open stone chamber, a room hewn out of the red bedrock in a perfect square. Lamps glowed bright, yet without flame, in the corners and along the walls. Tall, roughly hewn stone figures filled the room. She sniffed. They didn't smell like trolls. If they *were* trolls, no ready explanation for their stony state came to mind, protected as they were in this sunless room, deep underground.

On the far side of the chamber was a heavy ebony door. Memories flashed; she'd shuffled across this space, arms bound, with Juri and Dagmar beside her. Drott Ulf stumbled in the dark just ahead, and Earl Harald, as ever her chief tormentor, spoke in her ear from behind, his voice heavy with scorn, "Look what you've done now, girl." Then darkness, her last memory before waking up in the sorcerer's blood-soaked lair.

"He brought us into the keep this way," Runa whispered. "But these stone giants are different now."

"How so?"

"A pair stood under each lamp, against the wall. Now, they bar the way through the room."

Paolo hobbled around the nearest statue, craning his neck to look up at its carved features. "Old-fashioned. Auritrean-Revival style, I'd say, but . . ." He moved back and considered it from a new angle. "Not of the villa's era, at all. My great uncle preferred . . ."

She paid the lecture only half a mind and wound her way among the figures toward a small rectangle chiseled into the room's back wall. A blocky statue in flowing robes guarded the way, the figure at least half again as tall as Runa. Certainly not a troll, she decided, but rather an image of a troll fashioned from white granite. "Hail, Brother Granite, blessed and strong, eldest child of the mountain," she said in the ancient tongue as she bowed in the customary manner. The granite remained silent. In fact, it felt dead or at least drained of its life marrow.

"What curses . . ." She studied the form's carvings; perhaps runes bound the granite figure, and she could release it from the sorcerer's geas. Deep grooves suggested a human face, and cuts about the jaw resembled a beard. Its neighbors were of a similar style, but different in the details, some with a hint of a stony smile, others with trowel and mortar board or stonemason tools clutched to their chests. "How can I free you? Can you provide some sign?" The stones, however, were silent.

Runa looked again at the chiseled rectangle that had drawn her across the room in the first place. Marks were incised within it. "Look, a runestone. Perhaps it's the curse." She reached toward the glyphs to learn what they had to say about the room.

"Don't touch anything," Paolo said just as her fingers brushed the wall.

The white granite giant, its stone so dead a few moments earlier, shuddered and opened its eyes. Slowly at first, then faster and faster, it pushed her, while its fellows, also awakened, beat their stone hammer and chisel in a deafening rhythm on the chamber wall. Yet the granite *was* dead, the figures' movement an unnatural abomination. Damn that sorcerer, Runa thought, he murdered the very stone face of the mountain and summoned restless shades to inhabit these shards.

Paolo shouted nonsense above the din of the statues' hammers, "They're automatons. Look for the power switch."

"What?" Runa shoved at the statue, shouting, "Back, shade. Release Brother Granite now." It tottered a moment, then righted itself, and blinked its eyes as it advanced on her. The statues at work on the wall had created a shallow recess in the bedrock, and the shade that haunted Brother Granite's lifeless body herded her toward it. More possessed statues hemmed her in, jostling and nudging her. She took but a moment to ground and center her marrow then pushed out her will with a gestured rune and command, "Cease, shades. Leave this place."

The statues did not obey, continuing to shove her toward the niche in the wall. Brother Granite clasped the revolver's baldric in its thick stone fingers and pulled it over her head. "It's mine," she shouted, panicked to give up this bit of Paolo's technologia. She struck the figure, unfocused, cutting her hands on the stone.

"Find it yet?" She heard him as though from a great distance, his voice echoing around the chamber and bouncing off the poor, possessed granite statues. "It might be a toggle. Or a push button."

The air thick with stone dust, Runa coughed and sneezed as the granite giants pushed her into the crypt they'd built. They layered mortar on stone with their trowels to fashion a wall. She tried once more to shove them away but had neither the strength nor the space for leverage. Her vision obstructed by the growing stone wall, the room's cold lights winked out. "Help!" she coughed into the darkness.

Thurs/The Giant

THE GIANT IS THE MOUNTAIN, THE SKY'S EXPANSE, AND THE CURSE OF THE PRIDEFUL.

Freki's Edda, Aett Thurs, Stanza One

D odging the sharp hammer-on-chisel blows, Paolo probed the nearest automaton's chinks and crevices, the typical location of power switches. "Bloody engineers," he murmured but couldn't help but admire the subtle design. Automatons were generally made of metal and glass with an obvious clockwork power source. These appeared to be granite, of all things. Waldo barked at them furiously, nipping at their heels with, of course, no effect at all.

Paolo thought he heard Runa speak and looked across the room just as three automatons shoved him against the wall, their chisel-and-hammer blows dangerously close to his eyes. "Halt," he sneezed as stone dust filled his nose. He twisted, turned, and ducked their blows, all the while commanding, "Automaton, halt," but they didn't respond. His scabbard dangled at his side, entangled and useless, and he struggled to unlatch his sabretache to access his pistol. "Automaton, stop." He wracked his brain for every command phrase he'd ever heard or read. "Disengage—Stand down—Cease," he shouted. What powered them, he hadn't a clue. If he could just turn one off and take it apart.

"Any luck yet?" he called to Runa but was dismayed to see her rapidly disappearing behind an automaton-constructed wall. "No—" he yelled as he retrieved his pistol and fired its shot. The lead ball hit an automaton's neck and chipped off a tiny bit of stone before ricocheting around the room, narrowly missing Paolo. At first the automaton continued to press her into the niche, but as a crack slowly spread around its neck, movement slowed, then halted. However, the rest of the automatons continued their work, aiming to seal her behind a wall.

She has my other primed pistol, he thought. "Shoot," he shouted as automatons continued to shove him. "Shoot the neck with the pistol."

His shot spent and no time to reload, he pounded at the automatons with the gun. He switched from Auxumic to the few command words he knew in Ertz and even the invaders' language, Voxkllic. They still didn't react.

While he fought and shouted, they'd pushed him into a niche. A crypt, he realized, and walled him in chest high. His hands bloody from beating on stone with the now bent-and-broken pistol, he put all his strength into leaping up to swipe at the nearest automaton's jaw. He heard a snap of bone, and pain shot down his right arm. But a small scrap of paper fell out of the stone figure's mouth, and the automaton paused, blinking at him. Its hands fell to its side. Paolo was speechless, but only for a moment. "Their mouths. Hit the jaw," he shouted. "The power switch is in the mouth."

He took his own advice and climbed up the half-finished wall to be within striking distance of one of the figures' jaw. His blows failed to stop it, so he probed its mouth, mindful of chomping teeth. The automaton did, indeed, hold a paper slip in its mouth, and as Paolo dislodged the command code, it stood down. He made quick work of the other two in his immediate vicinity, then ran across the room to Runa. But she was sealed in a crypt, an affinity reaction diagram incised on its wall.

Paolo tapped. "Sir, are you well? Signal, please." Even as he spoke, he was shocked to see the rough stone and wet mortar transform into a smooth, cool iron surface. Although he didn't recognize all the symbols in the equation, he thought it described that new method to purify metals covered in the senior alchemy seminar, the one he hadn't taken yet. Whatever made the reaction work, it directed the iron molecules of the hematite bedrock to loosen their bonds with the calcium, silicate, and other earth elements to transform into the iron wall before him. A sizeable sand mound was piled on the ground. Good to know conservation of mass was still the law in this accursed place.

The automatons that had been on Runa began to chisel a new crypt beside hers and nudge him toward it. He pounded the iron wall and shouted, "Runa," only pausing to leap at the automatons' jaws to pluck command codes from their mouths. At last, they all powered down.

Exhausted, he slid to the floor and crouched in the rubble. "What do I do now?"

Waldo, who spent the battle alternatively barking and whimpering before the stone attackers, licked his face.

Paolo fished one of the automatons' papers out of the heap of broken stone. It had writing on it. A quadratic function, it appeared, with variable symbols he'd never seen before: the command code, possibly. He creased and folded the paper, idly fashioning a tiny horse. What he needed was some ordnance. Crushing the paper horse into a ball, he said aloud, "It couldn't mean much more than, 'I'm your master. Obey me.'"

He had so little time. *She* had so little time. Assuming the space held 500 or so liters of air, she'd survive perhaps an hour. Paolo snapped open his pocket chronometer, miraculously unbroken save for a cracked crystal. Nearly two in the morning.

In a fit of pique, he shoved the paper ball into the nearest automaton's mouth, a blue-veined marble model, which had toppled to the ground in the fight. "We must get her out of there." He thought for a second the automaton's eyes glinted, but he realized it was just a trick of the flickering light.

If he only had more black powder. Much, much more black powder. And a cannon. And shot. And a fuse.

He looked in his pouch. It held five paper cartridges of shot and black powder, the same as the last time he'd looked. An idea began to glimmer. Suppose, rather than propel a shot against the wall, the powder could be made to propel the wall against itself? Like mining engineers used to excavate precious-metals ore? That sort of charge would take considerably less powder.

Paolo dragged himself back up the stairs and staggered down the hallway. He needed a canister. He stumbled into the kitchen and raided the pantry, locating a tall cylindrical cookie tin and a small funnel he could jam, wide end first, into the canister.

As he plopped down at the kitchen table to work, the room swam before his eyes. He'd persisted on pure battle frenzy; suddenly all the emotions he'd tamped down—his anger at the king, hatred for Andries, and ardor for Runa—rose up and shouted, "Enough."

His excitement drained onto the floor in a puddle, though he tried to will the strength to push through. Paolo rested his head on his arms, which were folded against the table's battered oak planks, and watched huge snowflakes drift against the windows and block the gray light. He felt so tired. His hand throbbed, his leg ached, and his neck wound burned. Gray light. Morning coming. Which meant . . . something. Rest, just a moment. Then go on, stronger. He closed his eyes, but Waldo would have none of it. The dog growled and pulled at his boot.

"Master, you promised her."

"Wh—what?" Paolo roused himself. "Now you can talk again? I'm really quite poisoned, I am." He thought on the remedy Runa'd made him drink, a bat-venom antidote she brewed just for him with her own hands. What a wonderful person. He'd certainly never known anyone like her. And he did feel better after her treatments, just weak and . . . so . . . sleepy.

"You promised. It's nearly dawn."

From the forest outside he heard the faint chirping of birds. Yes, he thought, nearly dawn. While the room was still cloaked in shadow, the quality of the darkness had changed. Dawn. Which had some significance. He bolted upright. "Dawn." Andries' new power, the power Runa claimed he'd stolen from her drott, took full effect at dawn. Success, at least according to her . . . unique . . . beliefs, depended on the mage's defeat before dawn.

The hound barked and pulled at his jacket sleeve. It came off from the shoulder in his mouth.

"Very well, dog. When I'm killed, the king's alliance plan will fail." He picked his sleeve up off the floor. "How deluded am I? He'll find someone else to marry Earl Marta. Or Mother will adopt one of their minor nobles. Or Papa will broker an exchange of wild beasts and botanical specimens."

No one had ever depended on him the way Runa did this night, not even his artillery unit. He liked it, he thought as he prepared the canister charge. Paolo sat back and ate the tin's stale cookies as he inspected his creation.

It should work. He hoped it would work. The base of the cylinder was filled with air, separated from the powder by the funnel, which created an inverted wedge in the upper end of the tin. He'd packed the wedge with all the black powder in his cartridges. A stout length of twine served as a fuse, snaking out from under the cookie tin's lid. He sealed the canister as best he could with some gooey pine resin and a few carpet tacks.

The trick would be to place it close enough to the wall. "Let's go, Waldo. We've a friend to rescue and a mage to kill."

As he stood to leave, Paolo felt a low rumbling through the floor. Real movement, not a bat-venom hallucination. And not just the floor. The whole room vibrated: Painted plates rattled on their wall hooks. Glass jars of canned fruit, deployed on a high shelf, crashed to the floor, one by one. A thrumming noise accompanied the shaking. But whatever Andries was up to, first they had to rescue Runa. She might still be alive, he told himself. Still a chance.

Waldo bayed as they rushed from the room and found themselves in yet another dark passageway. Paolo'd lost the lantern in the battle of the automatons and could see nothing at all.

"Find the crypt," he urged the dog. "You know her scent." But Waldo wandered the halls in circles, sniffing and sneezing. The walls seemed to disappear whenever touched, only to reappear a few feet away. As he descended the familiar central staircase, he felt it move, the woosh of air cool against his face as the stairs slid around to an entirely different angle. Every corner they turned sent them further from the crypt and drew them closer to the gods-awful din, as if the building herded them along. Up ahead, he could see a diffuse light. Yes, definitely, a yellow-green glow in the near distance.

Peeking around a corner, Waldo growled and then backed away. When Paolo looked for himself, he saw an open doorway; the room beyond it shimmered like a mirage.

Sabre drawn, he burst into the room as fast as his shaking legs could run, Waldo at heel. Despite the green-tinged smoke enfolding the room, he recognized the place: the gathering hall. Dozens of hunters, servants, and dogs—even a horse or two— would have ample space to prepare for a day's sport or relax in the evening over cards and wine. Trophies and ancestor portraits still hung on the walls, but most of the antique furniture was gone.

However, overwhelming the room was a steam engine, at least twenty times larger than any model Paolo had ever seen. It rumbled and hissed, its vibrations shaking the whole villa.

Mergr/Marrow

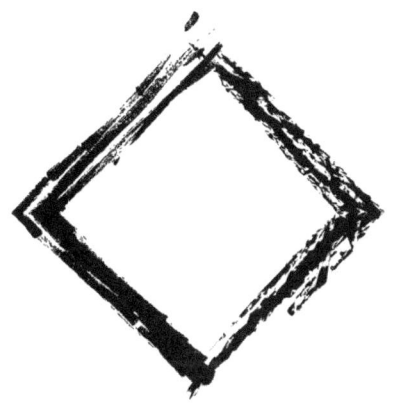

MARROW IS THE BONE'S HEART, LIFE'S QUICKENING, AND THE KINDRED'S BOND.

Freki's Edda, Aett Mergr, Stanza One

ndries' back ached. Hunched over a credenza-turned-laboratory bench, he'd checked and rechecked his calculations for hours. He stretched, rubbed his eyes, and glanced at the night sky framed by the hall's high windows. It was still dark, and a few snowflakes floated in through the open casements, but birdsong announced dawn's approach. Almost time. Where was the prince?

He strode over to his opus magnum, the extraction-rejuvenation chamber: A massive brass cylinder lined with two inner rings of copper coils, which rotated at high speed to produce an electromagnetic field.

He'd spent days sequestered inside the chamber, assessing the device's leg room and its upholstery's comfort. The cylinder was secured horizontally on the long feasting table. Abutted to the device's open end was a narrow but well-padded bed on which the subject must recline. Then he simply slid the subject, bed and all, into the magnetic field to perform the procedure. It had worked to perfection.

An amber glass reservoir hung beneath the table, full of a cloudy liquid. The fluid swirled at his approach. Andries tapped the glass. "Soon, brave souls, soon. Your great work will begin." The liquid darkened, and red glimmers sparked deep in the vial.

He wiped a daub of oil off the brass surface. He leaned in close to fog the metal with his hot breath, then buffed away the condensation. Still holding the soft rag, he stroked the chamber's wide curves and traced the intricate pattern of the gleaming brass fittings.

The extraction-rejuvenation chamber was beautiful, but it was useless without power. The pliant insulated wires that connected it to the potent electric generator beckoned him, power licking his hand, skipping across his body, and tingling up his spine.

Of course, there would be no electricity without steam to move the generator's turbines. The behemoth boiler groaned as his automaton servants fed it a steady diet of green wood, which cracked and popped as it burned. Smoke poured from the stacks and hung in dark clouds among the hall's high rafters. Mist boiled out of the machine's seams to swirl and ebb around him. He shifted under the stinking weight of the wolf pelt he still wore as he opened the engine's steam inlet valve.

A voice, barely audible over the engine's din, floated in from the doorway. "Andries Gideonius—"

Paolo. The boy had arrived at last.

"Release Runa this instant."

The engine's cylinders trembled with the force of the pistons thrusting back and forth inside them. "Our time is near," he whispered, then followed the sound of Paolo's voice through the fog.

"By my royal writ extraordinaire I detain you in the name of King Gian," the prince said.

"You feel I abandoned you, all those years ago." Andries stepped from behind the engine. "I understand. I didn't *want* to leave. But the king—"

"What the . . . " Paolo's eyes followed the pistons' connections to crankshafts, to flywheels, to turbine. "A generator? It's enormous."

He chuckled. Oh, this boy and his love of mechanics. "Think of the power capacity."

The prince frowned. "I mean . . ." He turned away from the machines and stared at Andries. "Free her now. You will answer charges of murder, kidnap, and . . . and"—he gestured around the hall—"criminal trespass."

Andries strolled to the extractor-rejuvenation chamber. "Just let me show you this."

Paolo made to rush him but, feet held fast to the floor by an embedded electromagnetic snare, stumbled and fell. As he did, his sabretache flew open and a canister skittered across the room. It came to rest under the steam engine. "What the diavolo!" He struggled to regain his feet. "Release me."

"I'm sorry," Andries said, hurrying across the room to a tall china cabinet in which he'd housed the trap's power control. "The binding circle wasn't meant for you." He depressed a lever, and the glowing lights in the floor at Paolo's feet blinked and faded. "Son, you've held up quite well to the rigors of this night."

Paolo marched toward him. "I'm not your 'son.'"

Andries held up both arms and stepped back. "Well, at least I *am* your friend." Wounded, he whispered, "More than friend; I consider you the child I never had." Over the din of the boiler and the engine's thrumming, he discerned another sound: the boy's heartbeat. "Listen." He cocked his head. "Hear that?"

"No," Paolo grabbed him by the collar, "I can barely hear myself think in here."

"Your heart knows," Andries tapped the prince's chest, then pointed to the extractor-rejuvenation chamber. "Your path to power awaits."

"You've had fair warning." A blade appeared in Paolo's hand. "I'll start by opening less important veins, but you *will* bleed to death unless you release Runa"—he held the knife to Andries' nose—"right now."

The older man chuckled as he stayed the hand that held the knife. "Don't you question how readily you followed her here? She led you right to my door. Did you take even one moment to examine her intentions?"

Paolo looked a tad green.

"She's been working with me all along."

His grip loosened.

"Runa was—*close*—to me, back in Sumarheimr. I was perhaps her only friend."

"I . . . I . . . don't . . . believe you," Paolo said.

Andries took the opportunity to elbow his way out of Paolo's weakened grasp and then held up his hands in a gesture of surrender. "Hear me out first. I had to get you away from the front line, so I pushed Drott Ulf to pursue the alliance with Auxumia and centered the pact on your marriage to a Frekigardr earl."

Paolo's jaw dropped, and his grasp on the knife loosened. Black curls stuck to the sweat of his forehead. "Why would you . . ."

The engine radiated heat and filled the hall with steam and smoke. Andries wiped his brow of sweat and wolf-pelt blood trickling down his face. He pointed again at the extractor-rejuvenation chamber. "A gift. For you."

"What *is* that?"

Sauntering over to the chamber, Andries said, "The ways of the Frekigardr are primal. Barbaric, even. But they keep their 'marrow,' as they call their life force, in the family." He pulled the power switch up. "Their quiddity is valuable. You, my dear, dear boy, can be part of a modern, scientific method"—he patted the narrow bed—"to harness the Frekigardrs' power. With this device I can both collect a subject's strength and innate gifts and *infuse* another subject with them."

He glanced up at the windows. "It's almost dawn." Withdrawing his slide rule from his sleeve, Andries said, "Let's begin." He made a quick calculation, then traced the functional symbol for rotation and flung it at Paolo's knife. It flared green-gold then disappeared in the smoky recesses of the hall. The blade flew out of the prince's hand. As it spun across the room, he tackled Paolo and pinned him to the floor with his full weight.

Waldo howled and lunged at Andries. Again, he inscribed rotation in the air and sent the dog flying. The animal smacked into the stone wall with a heavy, wet clunk.

"You're dead," Paolo shouted. Thrashing about, his head butted the mage squarely on the chin.

At the sudden pain Andries gasp but pressed him even more tightly against the floor. "I offer you everything you've ever wanted: A general's sash? A seat at the council? The throne itself, perhaps?" He invoked a simple negation function, and Paolo's body sagged, limp and heavy. Cradling the prince in his arms, he half-dragged, half-carried him toward the extractor-rejuvenation chamber.

Nauðr/Prison

PRISON FETTERS THE BODY, CRUSHES THE HEART, AND DRAINS THE MARROW.

Freki's Edda, Aett Mergr, Stanza Two

Entombed in the crypt, Runa shivered. Ulf must have shared more lore with Andries than she ever realized. Or perhaps she herself had talked too much. She well understood what the utlendr had valued in the kindred: Wolf-Mother favors us. We are strong. But we are few.

She'd escaped him once; she'd do it again.

She crouched in the stone dust and willed herself calm, breathing out all thoughts of defeat and loosening the knot in her gut with each breath in. She conjured her connection to the earth, the deep roots that fed her marrow. Anchored in her body, Runa felt serene. Until thoughts of Paolo intruded.

He'd been angry with her, with respect and admiration tempering his irritation. Did he work to help her, even now? The daydream tempted her, but she bridled her thoughts. "I am *in* my body." Said aloud, she felt present. "Here. Now. Completely. Nowhere else. I must save myself."

Runa searched for any hint of light. She held her breath to better sense any wisp of fresh air. She stood and ran her fingers over every inch of the stonework chamber, to find the tiniest chink, the smallest . . . what had he called it? . . . "Power switch." She felt no mechanism embedded in the stone.

And there he was again. Her memory lingered on his brawl with the evil shades inhabiting the man-shaped stones. Paolo had fought as fierce as Waldo had promised, discovering the shades' weakness as he did so. She thought she heard pounding on the wall, then realized it was her heart. Runa willed it to relax, to slow itself into a natural rhythm.

She probed the chamber three times, at least. The air grew hot, stuffy, and close. Dizzy, she leaned against the stone. Paolo had joined her cause; was he of the kindred now? Could he get her out of this crypt? She listened for the slightest sound of excavation and heard nothing. She howled to push out her thoughts to him. She imagined for a second she could sense him, but of course not. He was a good man but only an utlendr. Not of the kindred. A man who followed her into peril and trusted her judgment. Thus, her responsibility, kindred or not.

The strength to tear down the wall could only come from inside her. She pricked her finger with the knife and traced the rune Bjarkan on the stones. Wolf-Mother, she prayed, my need is great. I invoke the oath between us. Merge our wills. Mingle our shapes. Ancestors, aid my cause.

Runa shed the borrowed shepherd's garb. Her heart, guided by Wolf-Mother, sought out the muscles, ligaments, and tendons that needed to stretch, grow, and change. Supported by her kindred's legacy, she pushed and nudged, *here* and *there*.

Once the change began, it was only a moment until wolf-shape took her. The niche's tight space was now even tighter. Yet she was stronger. She raked her claws across the smooth wall, her powerful limbs wasted without room to run and lunge. Runa pushed at the wall, again and again, until she curled, exhausted, on the crypt's tiny floor.

A tear dripped down her snout and onto her lips. She licked it away. Her predicament was her own fault; she'd touch the cursed runes in the stone chamber, awakening the shades. Worse, she could've learned of toggles and push buttons from Andries but had scorned his utlendr ways. And now they would all die. While the sorcerer, the drott's marrow coursing through him, would enslave the kindred, ally with the invaders Paolo was so concerned about, and surrender Frekigard.

Runa strained to hear the slightest noise from the outside. She imagined him working at that very moment to get her out. His fealty warmed her, even across the stone wall, but she had to wonder if his devotion was as delusional as the pinpoint flashes of light before her eyes, white, red, and green like fireflies in a summer meadow at the gloaming time.

She'd finally told him enough truth, she hoped, for trust. The stale air weighed down her eyelids. Most likely the shades had captured him, too. At the image of Paolo suffocated in an enchanted crypt, she jumped up. She heard tapping on the other side of the wall. "I'm here. Right here," she shouted before realizing that perhaps the sorcerer had come to fetch her out. She'd prefer to die in the wall than be part of his scheme. The niche took up a queasy spinning, and, spent from the sudden effort, she collapsed in an unconscious heap.

***

Fresh, cool air revived her. Runa blinked and found herself, still in wolf-shape, draped over the outstretched arms of a stone figure, who shuffled down a corridor. She jumped down, and the shade didn't try to stop her. It was not Brother Granite, but rather a blue-veined marble giant. "Thank you, friend." The stone felt drained and dead as before; perhaps a life spark remained hidden. "I knew the stone-folks' better nature would prevail over the sorcerer's trolldomr."

Her ears perked up at distant thrumming sound, low and unnatural. Her hunt for the sorcerer would not be easy or safe. She needed a plan.

101

She sniffed the air: smoke, the earls, and Paolo. As she followed the scent trail, the sound grew louder and was joined by clanking, banging noises.

As she turned a corner, she spied Brother Granite grinding along the corridor ahead of her and followed. He carried the weapon he'd stolen from her, still holstered in its baldric. He went through an open stone archway, and she paused to peep into a large room. It glowed with green-yellow smoke and radiated trolldomr. Metal clanged on metal and echoed through the hall, as if an invisible army battled within.

She heard Andries shout over the din, "—everything you've ever wanted: A general's sash? A seat at the council? The throne itself, perhaps?"

Runa quieted the impulse to attack immediately and moved forward for a better view. Bile rose to her mouth: Andries, dressed in a wolf pelt, Drott Ulf's pelt her nose told her, pinned a struggling Paolo to the floor, the larger man's hips holding him to the ground. Waldo, gravely injured, was curled up against the far wall.

As she slipped into the room, she heard a few words of unnatural command and saw the young man go limp. The sorcerer began to drag Paolo toward one of the room's many metal structures; "technologia," he would call them, she was sure. What work they did, she couldn't imagine.

Runa started to pounce at Andries but was unable to move more than a few inches in any direction. She found herself within a circle of light surrounded by runes inscribed on the floor. The runes' marrow—strong, ancient, and perverted into trolldomr—intertwined with a strange force that poured out of a glowing tube of light embedded in the flagstones. She felt strange as well. Against her will, the change from wolf-shape to woman had begun, every sinew in agony as it struggled against itself to knit the smaller, weaker structure.

He lowered Paolo to the floor and hurried over to her. "Welcome,

Runa. Just in time. I need you." She growled and snapped at him, distracted, though, by her fight against her body's change from wolf-shape. If she ever needed her full strength, it was now.

Andries hit her square on the snout with the thin trolldomr box he'd used to curse her when she'd first escaped his stronghold. At the sharp pain she saw stars and crumpled at his feet, the change to woman-form complete.

"With your help, I can make the essence-serum even more powerful before Paolo receives the treatment. He'll be the first of my legion. Its general, in fact." He pointed to the graying sky outside the high windows. "When the drott's power binds with mine, my command will be secured."

Brother Granite put her weapon on a table and ground across the room to grab Runa and drag her to a narrow bed, which lay end-to-end to a hollow brass cylinder on a table. Thin black tubes snaked around it and into a flask that dangled from the table's underside. The place reeked of the hunting troop—Harald, Juri, Dagmar, even Gunnar and the rest—all crying out to her for rescue. Yet she couldn't see them, as close by as they felt. The copper and zinc of the device and the sand of the glass tank offered no wisdom. They were cold and silent. Dead.

Other technologia filled the room, just as dead, but far from quiet. Each larger than a glacial bear, one growled, hissed, and spewed steam like a geyser, the other hummed and shook like a monstrous beehive. The three beasts seemed to be in an unnatural communication amongst themselves.

Brother Granite was set on feeding her to the brass cylinder. He strapped her to the bed, and it began to crawl into the technologia. "In a few moments," Andries said, "you'll realize fighting is pointless." The cylinder had inner rings of copper wire coils, which began to spin, thrumming louder and louder with random clanks and groans. "Try to lie still. It will be less painful."

Blue light appeared off the spinning coils and traced her body, head to feet, then feet to head. Runa's skin tingled, and her hair rose of its own accord. She was dying—skin, muscle, bone ripping asunder—and her marrow draining away.

She steeled herself against the theft as she twisted and turned to avoid the light, but she was strapped down tight. Through the tube's open end, she could see Paolo's weapon on the table where Brother Granite had left it. Andries hovered over her lieutenant, waving the trolldomr box around and muttering curses.

If she could just get away from this metal beast. With a quick prayer to Wolf-Mother, Runa summoned her wolf-shape. Her bones thickened, muscles bulged, and tough, fur-covered skin strained against the leather straps, which tore away from the bed. She sprang out of the cylinder.

Andries head jerked up, and their eyes met.

She snarled and planted herself firm, shoulders back, tail erect. She sensed how much he loved Paolo, but pride, ambition, and desperation enveloped him as well.

He plucked a dagger out of his prisoner's boot and pressed it to the young man's throat. "I've already won. Make me kill him, and I'll punish your people severely for my loss."

She saw no way to rip out his heart and still save Paolo. Her mind reached out to Wolf-Mother, all the ancestors, and down deep into the earth, source of all strength. "Guide my purpose." Runa leapt onto the table, crashing its stacks of books, papers, and instruments onto the floor. She grabbed the weapon in the woman-hands knitted that very moment.

Andries' mouth gaped as he stared at her.

She pointed the pistol at him and squeezed the lever as Paolo had taught her. A report echoed throughout the hall, and the suddenly hot metal clattered to the floor as she dropped the gun.

Blood dripping from his left upper chest, Andries staggered toward her. He brandished the knife in one hand, his trolldomr box in the other.

Runa jumped off the table to advance on him, snarling. Just as she pounced, Andries shouted a curse and gestured at her with the box. Glyphs flared and burned in the air. She flew across the room to crash into the wall and then slid to the floor next to Waldo. The room spun, and as all went black, she heard Paolo's voice, "Nooo . . ."

Siðr/Custom

CUSTOM IS THE WELL-WORN PATH, THE MOTHER'S FEAST, AND THE HEARTHSTONE.

Freki's Edda, Aett Dómr, Stanza Four

Paolo woke from . . . a dream? Or delusion? Whatever the vision's source, Runa was a wolf. The beautiful white wolf from the forest who'd spooked his horse. She was trapped behind a blue, glowing portal. The air brimmed with mortar fire, explosions, and the acrid smell of gunpowder. He shouted to her but couldn't make her hear him over the din of battle. Then she leapt through the luminous ring. He heard gears grind and a gun fire. Someone chanted the calculus, an infinitesimal expression, the words harsh and heavy.

And then by the gods' good graces, there he was, flat on his back in Andries' laboratory. Actually, the gathering hall of his own home, and a white wolf lay crumpled against the wall near his dog. "Nooo . . ."

At the sound of his voice, Andries turned back from the wolf. A blood stain spread across his tunic. In his right hand he clutched Paolo's favorite dagger, and, in his left brandished his slide rule. Paolo would never beat his old tutor at maths, so he snatched a stiletto from its sheath under his left arm and struggled to stand.

Sweat poured down Andries' face, and his snarl matched that of the wolf's head he wore as a hood. "Hardly a fair fight, son," he said, feinting left, then right. "I'm old and wounded."

"You've skills enough still. I'm wounded, too." And poisoned by bat venom, Paolo thought. The motionless white wolf, bleeding from the ears, eyes glassy, and tongue lolled out, silently rebuked him and demanded revenge. "Murderer," he spat, then charged.

"I don't want to hurt you." Andries sidestepped the attack.

Paolo stumbled into the hot steam engine and jumped back from the technologia. Something warm and wet dripped down his cheek. He wiped at the tears—but, no, it was blood; Andries had nicked him in the pass. He stared at the red smudge across his palm. One crimson drop. Of Yared blood. A thousand-year-old royal dynasty, roots deep and twisted; vital to Auxumia. "Traitor." He circled his opponent, drew closer to stab, then fell away from his old master's return thrust.

"Please see reason, son." The dark stain from Andries' shoulder was spreading across his shirt and down his sleeve. Blood soaked the slide rule in his hand and dripped to the floor.

Paolo darted to the left, then pivoted to jab at Andries' wound from the right.

The sorcerer scuttled out of reach. "You don't want to *actually* hurt me."

All too aware of dawn only a few minutes away, Paolo blundered toward the older man who hissed in his ear, "Trust me," as he tripped the prince and then sidled away. While Paolo scrambled to his feet, Andries, pale and sweating, panted, "We'll . . . collect . . . her essence"—he tossed his head toward the dying wolf—"before"— then leaned against the brass cylinder—"it's too late." He signaled an automaton and pointed at the chamber. "Bring her," he said as he checked his slide rule and adjusted some controls on the generator.

The air stirred, and energy crackled across the room. Paolo's hair stood on end as he made a final push to run at the traitor. But Andries had slid to the floor. Eyes glazed over, he whispered, "Not yet dawn?"

Gods, Paolo thought, he takes the drott's power to the grave. What that meant for Runa and her people he couldn't fathom but knew it could be nothing good. She had to consume the heart. Right now.

He dropped his stiletto and pried his knife from Andries' hand, then cut into his old master's left side. He plunged his hand under his ribs and up into his chest, then yanked out a pulsating ball of tissue: the still-beating heart.

He ran to the white wolf: Runa, somehow wondrously transformed. Blood had clotted in her ears and mouth. He cradled her crumpled body in his lap. She didn't stir. "No, not yet." He held the heart to her open mouth, dripping blood onto her tongue. "Here it is," he said. "Damn you, eat it." But she was motionless.

By the gods, he'd *make* her preserve her people's legacy, if it was the last thing he ever did. He cut off a chunk of the heart and chewed the flesh well, then forced the meat bolus into her mouth. However, with all the stroking of her throat in the world, he couldn't make her swallow. He lay his ear against her chest and willed a heartbeat. He thought he heard it— more like felt it touch his own heart—but at last had to admit she was dead.

The first ray of dawn glinted off the windows, high overhead. The power could not be lost. But if he took on this task, would the power even be accessible? Well, there was only one way to find out. He might be killed trying to return the drott's essence to Runa's people, yet he'd risk it.

The blood's smell filled his senses, and calm descended on him: The focus of battle, when a soldier ceases to be an individual person and becomes part of a bigger, and deadlier, cause. Paolo lifted the heart to his own mouth. His canines tore into the muscle, the copper tang of blood mingled with an earthy essence that reminded him of Runa: grounded and bright. And ancient. He poured his anger and grief into ripping the heart apart with knife, teeth, and fingers. He consumed it entirely, then sat next to her, stroking her head, as sunlight splashed a rainbow prism across the great hall's stone floor. It fell upon a pile of wolf pelts, and he remembered her first charge to him. It had sounded ridiculous at the time, but now, a solemn duty. He had promised to return to the hearts among the trees and wrap them in the pelts.

A familiar whine interrupted his musings. Waldo had crawled over to Runa to lick the wound on her head. Paolo tousled the hound's ears as he swallowed past a sudden lump in his throat. "Old friend, I thought you were done for."

Waldo climbed into his lap and attended to the cut on his face. "Enough, enough," Paolo said, "I'm glad to see you too." He pushed the dog away and stood up. "Guard her a bit."

Waldo woofed softly and wagged his tail.

"She gave me a final order. Some sort of honorific of her people, I'll be bound."

***

Heavy-laden with wolf pelts, Paolo struggled through the snowdrifts back to the ward Andries had set as a barrier to the villa's grounds. As he approached the first dangling heart, a loud explosion in the distance cracked the air and sent flocks of birds flapping and cawing from the trees. He dropped the pelts and turned back toward the villa just as a second, even louder, volley erupted. "Puckle me." Perhaps the charge that he'd misplaced in the fight had detonated. Well, that was a puzzle. He'd never lit the fuse. Could the steam engine have exploded?

Normally he'd be pleased the improvised ordnance had actually functioned as intended, but all he felt was angry: He'd left Runa's body in the villa. And his poor dog standing guard. "Andries Gideonius, may Diavolo chain you in the frozen pit for eternity." He wiped an angry tear and tried not to picture the ruin, instead focused on the first dangling heart and which fur most befitted it. He spread the pelt out on the snow.

Some sort of words should be said. He knew barely any Frekic, so he sang an old tune in archaic Auxumic, a ballad probably older than both Frekigard and Auxumia, as organized kingdoms, at any rate. It was about the mountain range his people called The Roof of the World. She'd called its peak the Glacier Giantess.

He wasn't sure what he expected to happen as he untied each leather thong and wrapped the heart in a skin, but the simple sense of release that embraced him was welcome.

The last heart-laden tree bordered a small glade, open to the morning sun. Paolo finished his task and plopped down to rest. He scooped up a handful of fresh snow to lap it from his palm. He felt remarkably well, physically, anyway, although he stank of black powder, blood, and batshit. Neither his broken hand nor thigh wound pained him, and his night's labors and sorrow had left him refreshed and strong. If only Runa . . .

"See, I did as you asked," he said as he glanced back on his work. He was surprised—yet somehow not surprised—to see, rather than a neat array of pelt-wrapped hearts precisely aligned among the pines, a troop of tall, broad-shouldered men and women blinking in the morning sun and struggling to move their limbs. They nuzzled and embraced until someone noticed him, shouted an alarm, and they all turned on him.

Bjarkan/
Wolf-Mother

 OLF-MOTHER IS THE
KINDRED'S GUARD, THE
YOUNG'S SUCCOR, AND
THE HEART'S DOOR.

Freki's Edda, Aett Dómr, Stanza Two

Waldo's boy had left the doors open. Cold wind whipped through the room, and the house creaked and swayed along with the trees. Waldo cuddled against Runa's body, whimpering like a pup determined to soak up his mother's warmth. He drifted off into a dream in which he climbed a tree to snatch at bats that dove, swooped, and bit him. He roused at a faint stirring in her chest. "Steady on, there. Don't be daft. Just my own tail wagging." But then he felt another thump, then heard a lubb-dupp. The doors of Runa's heart had opened and closed. He yelped and licked her face.

She blinked, then opened her eyes.

Dómr/The Judge

THE JUDGE IS THE RULER, THE MEASURE OF WOLF, AND THE SCALE OF RIGHT ACTION.

Freki's Edda, Aett Dómr, Stanza One

Struggling to sit up, Runa looked around for Paolo and the sorcerer. As best she could tell, she was alone with Waldo. She gulped, swallowing a lump of meat inexplicably in her mouth.

The cursed stone figures were quiet, abandoned by the shades that had possessed them, but the sorcerer's technologia looked ready to attack. One spouted steam and smoke and shook the entire room. Lightning arced out of another mammoth device, randomly striking the room's objects while it vibrated as if to fly apart. The third beast—Andries had tried to feed her to it—clamored like a bell as its concentric cylinders gyrated.

She began to feel stronger, somehow. She needed to find the sorcerer, kill him, and devour his heart: The heart that now beat with her drott's own marrow and the kindred's heritage.

She sniffed the steam-and-smoke-laden air. Human blood and wolf marrow mingled and made it difficult to track either one. Although at least one source of blood was easy enough to find; the dead sorcerer, still wrapped in Ulf's hide, lay in a dark, sticky pool. She found the venom antidote in Andries' pocket.

But the sorcerer's heart had already been cut out, and Paolo was nowhere to be found. What in the whole of Wolf-Mother's realm had he done now?

Waldo limped over to the dead sorcerer and growled.

"You're right," she shoved the body to unwrap it of the hide. "We'll bring the drott's mortal remains with us." She could still sense the earls, even hear them cry out to her. Where were they?

Her eyes lit on the large amber tank attached by clamps to the underside of the brass cylinder. From it, the earls howled for release. Runa ran to the earls' imprisoned marrow, pushed at the reservoir with her snout, but couldn't move it.

Wild, confused, and alone amid the smoke and noise, the howling of the wind, and even more frantic howling of the earls' wolf essence, she reached out yet again for Wolf-Mother's grace and the ancestors' favor. Her change filled her heart and flowed through torso, legs, and paws. With sinews knit again into her woman-shape, her fingers twisted free the hot glass vial from the clanging brass cylinder, only to drop it.

The glass shattered on the stone floor, the spilled liquid twinkling like sun-soaked rain as the wind carried it away. She'd done all she could; the rest was up to the earls.

The technologia had grown quiet, Runa noticed, and the lightning storm amidst the hall's support trusses had ceased. However, she smelled the explosive powder that powered Paolo's mechanical weapons, as well as the smoke that poured off the largest of the beasts. It grew thicker by the second, an odor of scorched oil and hot metal rather than wood.

The wind moaned under the eaves, tugging at the slate roof. Waldo cowered at her feet. "Friend Storm may knock down the building before the beast does," she said to him. "You should leave this place." But he stuck even closer as she wrapped herself in the drott's hide for some warmth against the cold gusts and retrieved the vial of venom remedy.

Coughing, they crawled along the floor to the open doors. She climbed down the trees with the dog whining on her back. On solid ground at last, they were crouched, sucking in the clean, frozen air, when a roar erupted above them, followed in short order by another, even louder, retort. The ground shook, and they burrowed into a deep snowdrift, Ulf's pelt a shield against the sharp fragments of wood, metal, and glass that rained down on their backs.

The ruin of Andries' stronghold swayed in the upper branches of the trees, now held there by fading trolldomr alone. "Run!" Runa shouted at Waldo. But the ground was littered with broken glass, burning chunks of wood, and twisted metal, and they had to pick their way across Andries' battlefield.

At a safe distance, they dropped to the ground to rest. Black smoke marred the bright blue of the sky, but a brisk north wind scrubbed away at the sorcerer's blight.

"Good morrow," she greeted the sun. "I seek the earls; what remains of them, at least." The rays picked up a set of deep tracks across the snow-covered garden. Runa studied them, smelling and tasting the snow. Paolo, heavily laden. She hoped that meant he'd found the earls' pelts and was headed to the heart ward.

As she walked, she reflected on the night. She was . . . fond of her lieutenant, but he had to explain what had become of the sorcerer's heart. She traipsed through the snow, lost in her thoughts, while the small dog jumped over the drifts to stay at heel. As she approached the ward, her heart leaped as she recognized voices up ahead, speaking Frekic. The earls. At least Paolo had done as she had asked with the pelts.

"Andries—" That would be Harald.

"Yes, I remember. He escaped—" Dagmar, a skilled silversmith also respected for her prowess with the bow, had been particularly enraged at Andries' betrayal, seeing as she'd taken him in as husband.

A muffled voice, Juri, perhaps, said, "The drott called out the search party—"

Harald continued, "The way was clear, and we entered a rocky gorge . . ."

Their voices fell silent. Runa froze, and Waldo tucked his tail between his legs and bolted into the woods.

"Where's our drott, utlendr?" said Harald. "And where has that Runa hidden herself?"

The earls were weak. At their most dangerous. She had to distract them from Paolo.

"Runa is here." She stepped from behind the trees into the glade. She couldn't even see Paolo in the crowd of Frekigardrs looming over him.

The troop, except for Harald, forgot the young man in an instant and bound toward her. Would they embrace her or attack?

She lowered her head in submission, then thought of the danger. Instead, she raised her eyes to glare at the earls. She threw back her shoulders and showed a hint of teeth.

Dagmar's brown eyes flashed, and she ran at Runa but stopped short. She tilted her head and sniffed. "We've been cursed," she said without her usual disdain. The other earls hung back behind her.

"Most horrible dream." Juri's dark brown skin, sweaty despite the cold, was ashy. He shook his head as if to fling the memories away. "I still—"

"Aye, I thought I was flayed and hung out to dry." Gunnar, oldest and far from wisest, dropped to the ground and huddled there, his gray beard dirty and tangled with leaves and twigs. He looked up at Runa, a bit of the old twinkle in his blue eyes. "Speaking of dry, you don't happen to have a brew on you?"

The earls, it seemed, had decided not to attack, and their voices fell away to a distant murmur. She smiled, happy, just happy, to see Paolo again.

But Harald hadn't approached with the others. He continued to stare at her, chest puffed forward and stance wide-legged. He shoved Paolo toward her, and the chattering knot of earls backed away. "Talk, sorcerer," Harald said to him. "What did you do to us? Where is our drott?"

Runa swallowed back a whimper and barked, "This man is not a sorcerer. Or our enemy. He has, in fact, released you from Andries' curses."

Harald growled in Paolo's ear, "If you've cursed her, too, I'll—"

"I am not cursed." She tugged him away from the earl's grasp and faced Harald, shoulders straight, lips curled back, eyes ablaze.

The rest of the party backed away as Harald flexed his shoulders and growled at Runa and Paolo. He sniffed, and suspicion dawned on his face. "I *smell* Ulf. And see you wrapped in Ulf's pelt. What have you two done?"

Paolo launched his full weight against the bigger man's chest. Harald slid in the wet snow and toppled to the ground, pulling Paolo with him. Within an instant, he produced a blade and pressed it to Harald's throat. "Just *think* to hurt Runa, and you die."

"You two, cease," her voice echoed through the snowy woods. "Paolo, unhand him. Earl Harald, just listen a moment."

Paolo obeyed but returned Harald's sniffs and growls one for one.

"Quiet," she said.

They stood silent, stealing wary glances back and forth, spines stiff and chins jutted forward. Harald was a burly ginger two heads taller than Paolo. Dark, green-tinged smudges creased Paolo's eyes, and his face and hands were covered in cuts. Both men were weak of marrow and exhausted. They couldn't long resist once again snarling at each other.

Runa cleared her throat, and they looked back to her.

Paolo saluted. "Sir."

"Girl, explain yourself," Harald said.

She bared her teeth and growled, narrowing her gaze. The morning sun peeped over the trees, shining in Harald's eyes. He squinted and raised his hands to shield his face.

Runa turned to the other earls. "You, blessed by Wolf-Mother, give her and our ancestors thanks." A few earls snarled at her. "Ulf is dead, murdered by that creature, Andries, trusted as a friend by our drott and the kindred." She unwrapped Ulf's pelt from her shoulders and unfurled it on the ground. "More proof, if you need it, of what cruelty he performed."

The troop sniffed and stroked the drott's remains. Their kenning reverberated through the woods to be taken up by bird call then passed along to the mountains. The whole of the land shook with grief.

Harald, dry-eyed, shouted, "And his heart?" He glanced at the other earls.

"The sorcerer stole the drott's marrow," she said. "And the sorcerer is now dead."

Dagmar spoke the question in all the earls' hearts. "The lineage is lost, then? Our new leader will hold nothing from the past?"

Runa willed her voice calm. "With Wolf-Mother's blessing, our ancestors' favor, and the kindred's help, the drott can build a new lineage." A task to occupy their minds was in order. "Let us build a pyre for Ulf's pelt as is the custom due a great chieftain. If any remnant of the sorcerer's body can be found in the stronghold's wreckage, drag it into the woods. Our little sisters and brothers can feast upon it."

"Yes," said Dagmar, wiping her face of tears. "Let the sorcerer feed the foxes and ravens."

"The least he could do," said Juri.

"Drink honor to the good old drott," said Gunnar. "He was a wise one until he wasn't."

The weeping earls trudged back toward the ruins. Harald growled once or twice at Runa but then turned and trailed after them.

"Hurry," she called to the earls as she ran to Paolo. She stood close, so close she could smell Ulf on him, even if the others hadn't quite figured it out.

He'd done it. Consumed the sorcerer's marrow and hence the drott's. Yet she couldn't let the bat venom poison his heart. She handed him the blue glass vial. "Drink this."

"You were dead," He smiled. "But now . . ." His gaze flitted over her woman-shape, his expression admiring yet concerned.

In her hurry to escape, she'd forgotten to clothe herself. Likely an important custom in Skogr Utlendr, she thought. I must remember that.

"Aren't you cold?" He shrugged out of his tattered jacket and tied it around her waist with his sash like a kilt.

She pointed to the bottle. "Drink it now." She pitched her voice quiet and neutral.

He grinned and toasted her then quaffed it in one gulp and tossed the flask over his shoulder. "Not to mention, you changed into a wolf." He shook his head. "A wolf. And this—all this . . ." he waved his arms at the bloody tree branches—"magic. It's unbelievable. Wonderful . . ." His marrow could stand still no longer, and he ran and jumped high to snatch a pine cone from a bough.

Runa steeled herself to kill him. "One mystery at a time." Despite their rough start, she'd come to like him. "Bashed, not dead." Perhaps the drott's essence hadn't yet knit with his own. Surely there was some other way . . .

He lopped back to her through the slush and tapped her chest. "*You* had no heartbeat. I checked. Many times."

She shrugged. He was making things impossible. "I won't deny I was gravely injured. But I'm made of strong stuff." Runa sniffed him. "As are you now, apparently." Was this pleasant expression—open, happy, friendly—a mask? "When did you decide to steal our kingdom?"

"What?" His surprise seemed genuine. A skilled actor, too.

"From the start, back in the forest? Or after your old mentor spoke to you?"

He stepped back. "I never——"

"Yet, by all rights, you are now the drott of Frekigard." She tried to keep the anger out of her voice. He was as ambitious to rule as any utlendr. "Why else would you eat the heart?"

"Oh." Paolo lowered his head and sank to his knees in the snow. "I tried to make you eat the wizard's heart, but you wouldn't swallow even one bite. You *were* dead." He looked up at her. "You were intent, weren't you, to not only deny Andries the drott's power, but also to return it to your people?"

Runa knew what she *wanted* to believe. She searched his face again for any sign of deceit. She saw bruised olive skin, blood-spattered stubble along his jaw, and dark circles under his eyes. He smelled of adoration. For her. And hurt feelings. His sweat held no hint of lies or schemes. Although, by consuming the sorcerer's heart, he had seized the kindred's leadership. How could she trust him?

Paolo offered her a knife. "Now take my heart and become your people's leader." His half-smile didn't hide his gritted teeth as he looked away. "Waldo recommends you highly."

The wind carried a whispered warning. The earls, led by Harald, were marching back. No, running back.

Runa batted the knife out of Paolo's hand and dragged him to his feet. "Go home. Now."

"Why?" He started to turn and see what had her attention, and she threw her arms around his neck and pulled him close in a tight embrace.

"Here we must part," she whispered in his ear. His arms tightened around her, pressing her hips against his own. Her skin tingled as his devotion caressed it. His body was warm and solid. Dependable. And dangerous. What he'd done would get them both killed.

"Don't you"—Paolo brushed his lips, dry, split, and cracked as they were, across her forehead—"need"—a painful, yet pleasant wave of urgency flooded her groin, encompassed her body, and drowned her suspicions—"the drott's essence I carry?"

He'd consumed her kindred's lineage along with the sorcerer's heart, and it poured over her in his kisses. His lips lingered on her closed eyelids, then the tip of her nose. She nuzzled his face, her need mounting as his beard's stubble scratched her cheek.

A dull ache began to throb deep inside her. A spark of her marrow, the potential for new life, flickered into existence. Runa gulped and pushed him away. From the forest she heard barking and rustling among the underbrush. She pointed as a black stallion crashed through the tree line, Waldo nipping at his legs. "Quickly, now. Take your dog and horse. Go home."

"I don't—"

"Go back to your family and obey them in all things."

"A kiss and good-bye, eh?" His eyes were full of reproach.

Runa had much to learn of Skogr Utlendr. And so much to teach Paolo about Frekigard. She couldn't wait to begin. However, she had to first placate the earls. "Trust me."

"I want—"

"I know what you want," she said, kissing the pink scars on his face. "It will be well. Now go." It hurt to send him away. But the earls—

"How—"

"Trust me." Runa breathed a silent prayer that she had made the right choice. And that he wouldn't look back.

He sulked off toward the woods, whistling for his animals.

Runa bolted toward the earls. Harald led them, Ulf's pelt held high across his arms. He tossed it at Juri, then advanced on her. The rest of the earls gathered around them.

"I accuse Runa of treason," Harald said to the earls, "and trolldomr. Always cursed and resentful, she hired mercenaries of Skogr Utlendr to attack our drott."

She fought her dueling impulses—to run for a hiding place or grovel for forgiveness—and willed pride in her stance and calm in her voice. "You're mistaken, Earl Harald. You trusted Andries as much as the drott did." She approached each earl in turn to stare deep into their eyes. "We were all deceived." Dagmar bit her lip and lowered her eyes, and Runa nuzzled her face to whisper, "You, most of all."

"However," Runa continued, forcing her voice and will toward the other earls, "this is not the time—"

Harald's attack from behind caught her off guard, but her fall pulled him down into the snow as well. She yelped and struggled out of his grasp, then turned on the man as she jumped back up to her feet. The earls scrambled out of the way. "Who'd of thought it?" Gunnar said to Juri. "Harald fighting Runa, of all people, to be the next drott."

Harald, too, quickly regained his footing and advanced on her.

Panicked, she ran from the taller, heavier man. "I don't want to fight you, Earl Harald. I've no ambition—"

"You've schemed this whole time"—he lunged and caught her by the shoulder as she tried to twist away—"with sorcerers."

Runa wasn't a fighter. She scanned the circle of earls for any place of shelter or escape, but they closed ranks. Most cheered Harald's lunges and blows and pushed her back toward him when she strayed too far from his reach.

Harald grabbed her throat from behind and squeezed. The forest darkened, and lights twinkled, then shifted before her eyes. After a moment of struggle, she felt calm and at peace. "Now is your time," Runa heard Drott Ulf say in her heart. "Bind my marrow to your own." The earth steadied her, and Ulf himself as well as all the drotts from the past joined the ring of earls to cheer her in the battle.

She went limp, falling back against Harald's chest. His grasp on her loosened, and she twisted away. She dove to the ground and then grabbed his legs. Off-balanced, he fell.

"Ru-na. Ru-na," Gunnar cheered. "Take the braggart down, girl."

"Yes," Dagmar said, "You can do it."

With their good will joining the cheers of drotts long past, Runa jumped to her feet to face Harald, who'd already scrambled up out of the snow to tower over her. "I didn't *plan* to kill you," he said, "but I will."

Runa growled. She felt Wolf-Mother's favor as their marrows mingled. Her change took only seconds, and her wolf-shape felt bigger and stronger than ever.

"She . . . she looks like Ulf in his youth," Juri said.

"A bit, perhaps," said Gunnar, "but more like old drott Thor, back when I was young."

Harald stood dumbfounded, too shocked, it seemed, to concentrate on his own change. She advanced, bared her teeth, and growled again.

"Are you blind?" said Dagmar. "It's Wolf-Mother herself, come to fight for the girl." She knelt in the muddy, trampled snow. "Hail, Drott Runa."

Harald, apparently unable to channel his marrow into wolf-form, grabbed the knife Paolo'd dropped earlier. He slashed the air—"Stay back"—as he scuttled away.

Runa continued a slow advance. She darted left then right, yet always forward.

Gunnar, then Juri, joined Dagmar to kneel. "Drott Runa, Drott Runa," they chanted.

Harald swiped at her with the knife, but she grabbed his wrist in her teeth. She bit and shook his arm, blood dripping in the snow, as the man screamed, helpless. The knife fell to the ground. All the earls took up the call, "Drott Runa, Drott Runa."

"Yield. I yield," Harald said, flat on his back in the muddy snow. "Drott Runa."

Gipt/Gift

Gift is joy freely bestowed, blessing all and pleasing the ancestors.

Freki's Edda, Aett Thurs, Stanza Three

"Are you decent?" a female voice called from outside Paolo's pavilion. His cousin, Crown Princess Vanessa, had thrown herself into his wedding plans as if they were her own all over again. "Never mind decent," another female voice said, "Are you ready to get married?" Lady Sara, Vanessa's spouse, loved a party almost as much as the princess.

"Come in," he said. "I'm both decent and ready." He wished either were true. This wedding would end in his execution sooner or later. Which would at least put him out of his misery. Some mornings all that got him out of bed was Drott Ulf's marrow, knitting to his sinews more tightly each day.

The young ladies swept in to display their finery, the princess's crimson frock bringing a blush to her olive complexion and Sara's canary yellow gown warm against her brown skin.

Waldo bound toward them, dropped a ball at Sara's feet, and made a play bow. She leaned forward to scratch his head. "Not now, boy. You best be making yourself calm, or you won't be invited to the wedding."

"This uniform doesn't fit you at all," Vanessa said. She tugged at the sleeves as if that would somehow make them longer. "Haven't you something else to wear?"

Paolo had to agree; his jacket stretched and puckered across his chest, and the sleeves were inches too short. At least the too-short breeches didn't matter, tucked in as they were in his too-tight boots. "Not really. None of my clothes fit any better than this."

"He *should* wear his good uniform," Sara turned down the sleeves' cuffs. "There. Somewhat longer."

"It will have to do," Vanessa laughed. "Everyone will be looking at the bride, anyway." But then her face grew solemn. "This alliance is crucial," she said. "I know you were enjoying life in the army, reluctant to—"

"I understand my duty." He paced the length of the pavilion in two strides. I'll suffocate in here, he thought.

"Of course. You know what I mean. You've been wise beyond your years, let's just say that. I'm proud of you."

Sara dabbed her eyes—"We're all proud"—and blew her nose on a lacy kerchief.

With a commotion of footsteps and orders to "attention," the tent flaps flung open. "Is Vanessa in here?" King Gian burst in. "They've pulled a switch on us."

"What?" Vanessa, Sara, and Paolo said in unison.

"They've changed their minds. You're not to marry Earl Marta after all."

His heart rose, then sank. The drott in him pined for the high mountains and their kindred. And compelled him to bring the drott's marrow and Frekigard's lineage home. Although Paolo fully expected to be devoured as soon as the earls perceived what he had done with Andries' heart.

"But he's to marry . . . someone . . . today?" said Vanessa.

"Oh, yes." The king plopped down on a campstool, which creaked under his weight. "This is most irregular."

"You don't approve of the bride?" As far as Paolo could tell, the whole Auxumian government was ready to marry him off to make the best deal they could, regardless of whom the bride might be. "Or the match won't seal the alliance quite like you thought?"

An attendant appeared at the tent flap and bowed to the king. "Your majesty, it's time." He turned to Paolo, bowing again. "Your Grace, your bride awaits."

Paolo stepped out of the pavilion. Crows greeted him. The villa's rubble was mostly cleared, and all the dead trees carted away. Each shepherd on the mountain had gotten at least three cords of firewood. Paolo had already ordered many of the new replacement saplings, though he wouldn't be there to plant them, of course. He was about to be traded to Frekigard.

Snow clung to the garden's shady patches, but for the most part the melt dripped off the rocky outcrops and gurgled along the brook. Purple crocus and white snowdrop blossoms bask in the noonday sun.

He approached his mother, Lady Asha, his other father, Sir Fredrick, and the knot of courtiers and guests. They stood under a sheer canopy pitched beneath one of the few ancient oaks not destroyed by Andries. He recognized some of the bride's party—Juri, Dagmar, Gunnar—and nodded. Harald hadn't come, apparently. Just as well. They hadn't parted on the best of terms. Solemn faced, the earls returned his salute. Their leather cloaks were flung back against the warmth of the sun. Must still be cold in Frekigard.

Then he saw her. She stood apart from the other guests. His heart leapt up and caught in his throat. When she smiled at him, he heard his blood rushing through his veins. He heard everyone else's blood rushing through *their* veins. The sky was impossibly blue, the air smelled as sweet as honey, and the crows cawed as melodious as any bard.

Not entirely sure how he got there, Paolo found himself at her side looking down into her gray eyes. Over thigh-high leather boots her finely woven wool tunic matched the brilliant sky, and a band of linked silver rings that were nestled in her white-blonde curls sparkled in the sun.

His mother appeared at his elbow. "Your Royal Highness Drott Runa, may I present my youngest son, Prince Paolo Vitela Yared, Duke of Aufeer."

His face flushed at the pompous title. He braced himself for her laughter, but she inclined her head to Lady Asha, although she didn't take her eyes off Paolo. "Runa's sufficient, my lady," she said.

He wanted to gather her in his arms and kiss every inch of her face but made himself bow. "Runa. You honor our court."

"You look well, lieutenant." Her grin belied her formal response. "You're"—she looked him up and down—"taller."

"You know one another?" his mother said.

"We met, riding—"

"In the forest near here," Runa said.

Suddenly heartsick as he remembered the duty that had brought them all together this day, he glanced around the gathering. "Will you please introduce the bride?"

"Her Highness, I mean, Runa," Lady Asha flashed a tense, diplomatic smile, "values our alliance so highly she chooses to seal it herself."

The meadow lurched, and he grabbed Runa's hands to steady himself. He had no words, yet all the words stuck in his throat. "You-you-mean . . ."

"I thought I might let you help me again," she said.

Paolo barely registered his mother's shock as he folded Runa in his arms and whispered in her ear, "Sir, my heart is yours."

About The Author

Kathy lives and writes in St. Louis, Missouri, USA. Her hometown and its history inspire much of her fiction. When she's not thinking about how haunted everything is, she enjoys hiking, crafts, and cooking for her family. Follow her on all the usual social media. Kathy's blog, *Kathy L. Brown Writes: The Storytelling Blog*, lives at kathylbrown.com.

Her Sean Joye Investigations stories, *Water of Life* and *The Resurrectionist*, were published in 2019. Montag Press plans to release the first Sean Joye novel, *The Big Cinch*, in 2021. Her short fiction has most recently appeared in the St. Louis Writers Guild anthologies, *100th Anniversary Anthology* and *Love Letters to St. Louis*. Visit her website for links to all published works.

About The Typeface

This book's text is set in Baskerville, a serif typeface designed in the 1750s by calligrapher John Baskerville. The contrast between strokes, sharper serifs, and circular curved strokes all show the influence of the designer's calligraphy training. (https://en.wikipedia.org/wiki/Baskerville)

Two typefaces are used for display text. LTC Caslon is one of many Caslon revivals popular for setting printed body text and books. Caslon typeface was developed by William Caslon, a contemporary of John Baskerville, and appeared widely in books and periodicals from England and the United States. It was used for setting the American Declaration of Independence. (https://en.wikipedia.org/wiki/Caslon)

Mason Serif, designed by Jonathan Barnbrook, Émigré Foundry, is also used as a display typeface. Barnbrook was influenced by nineteenth-century Russian letter forms, Greek architecture, and Renaissance Bibles. The letter forms also evoke stonecutters' work, Freemasons' symbology, and pagan iconography, according to the Émigré Foundry website. (https://www.emigre.com/Fonts/Mason)

About The Runes

This book plays fast and loose with runelore; the story doesn't take place on our version of planet Earth, so while the runes look similar to ours, their names and/or meaning differ. These decisions were deliberately made to serve the needs of the story; I took poetic license and ran off with it.

Readers interested in actual runes can consult the following excellent references:

- Jónasson, Björn & Scudder, Bernard (trans.) (2014): *A Little Book About The Runes*, Gudrun, London.
- Thorsson, Edred (2012): *Runelore: The Magic, History, And Hidden Codes of The Runes*, Weiser Classics, San Francisco.
- Thorsson, Edred (2020): *Futhark: A Handbook of Rune Magic (rev. ed)*, Weiser Classics, Newburyport, MA.
- The Vikings of Bjornstad: Viking, Norman & Anglo-Saxon Reenactment website has an extensive English-Old Norse dictionary. https://www.vikingsofbjornstad.com/Old_Norse_Dictionary_E2N.shtm